Alice Dippleblack in

Flight

By
K. J. Bailey

Second Edition

ISBN: 978-0-9978858-8-0

Chapter 1

Earth & Fire

The four girls scoot away from the edge of the cliff instinctively, the slow gate of the distant titan sending rumbles through the earth at their feet. They watch in awe as the towering figure makes its way west to some unknown destination for some equally unknown purpose. It's triangular in shape, its peak very acute but it's body widening, though not greatly, further down. The tall trees of the dense expanse of untouched forest obscure whatever legs it uses for locomotion. The living mountain has no arms or other upper limbs that the girls can see, but so far away it's difficult to be sure. It slowly shrinks with each ground shaking step, the tremors lessening as well, giving the party the impression that it's heading northwest and away from them.

Alice Dippleblack finds herself taking rapid shallow breaths on the wildly unlikely possibility that deeper breaths might attract the colossal creature's attention.

From the corner of her eye she sees Danahlia

Smoothide nod beside her, "Yeah. Ya know, I didn't really mind the cave that much. Let's go back."

"Wow, what do you think it eats?" asks Kaliska Snowtail, the Chitali rising to her hooves as the titan reseeds further into the horizon.

"Unbelievable," murmurs Twinkaleni Orbear, the diminutive mouse girl rolling back onto her rump as if pushed by a strong wind, "Inconceivable."

Alice tears her eyes from the titan, tan in the morning sun, and looks to the Liguna standing to her taloned feet, "You wanna go back? But we just got here."

Danahlia pats Squiggles, the blood red juvenile dragon still alertly looking after the gigantic creature, as she passes to head for the steaming cave mouth they had just emerged from, "Yup. Call me whatever you want but I suddenly lose interest in places that have thousand foot tall monsters walkin' around."

Twinkaleni looks over to the lizard girl, tiny hands grasping bare pink feet while she rocks on her bottom in a a rare moment of childlike glee, "Not a monster, Danny. A *titan*."

Danahlia waves a negligent hand to the young Murin mage, "I hear the words and refuse to acknowledge a difference. No matter what you wanna call it, I'm callin' it dangerous. Did you see the size of that thing? It could crush us and not even know it."

Alice looks after the titan and reasons, "Well, it's gone now."

Danahlia searches the clear horizon, "Maybe, but what if it comes back? Or there's more of 'em?"

Kaliska's eyes widen, "More?"

Danahlia nods, "Why not, who knows what's out there?"

"Don't you wanna find out?" asks Alice, looking out across the great wilderness known only as the Wildlands.

The Gadara Mountain range the girls had passed through acts as Arsalia's and Feoria's northern border. The imposing natural barrier has prevented any further expansion by the nations and so the Wildlands remain a region unmapped, unexplored, and thus, largely unknown. Spotting a titan, creatures only said to have existed before Arsalia's founding, within minutes of reaching this mysterious place has peaked the naturally curious fox girl's interest.

Danahlia purses her lips at the sea of vibrant forest beyond their cliff, seemingly unscathed by the passage of winter. The brown skinned girl then turns back to the cave, "Nope, I'm good."

The others manage to get Danahlia to agree that at least a break is an order. The girls and Squiggles have a meal from their stores while they excitedly discuss their discovery. The usually well informed Twinkaleni surprises everyone by saying she knows very little about titans.

"As I imagine is the case for most," she says, head held high when the others express their shock, "Titans are only mentioned in Arsalia's earliest history and even then sources I have read coincided on only a few details. Most commonly,that titans are enormous, the largest living things ever recorded, though even 'living' may be inaccurate."

"It looked pretty alive. It was movin' and stuff," comments Alice, yanking a bit of jerky apart with her canine teeth.

Twinkaleni nods, "Indeed, and mind you this is only speculation on my part, but judging from what we just saw, I wonder if titans don't have more in common with elementals than living beings. This would require extensive observation and experimentation but to think we found them so-"
"Whoa, extensive and experimentation sounds like you wanna stick around and play with 'em," Danahlia interjects.

"Oh can we?" asks Kaliska a few half chewed leaves falling from her mouth.

Twinkaleni looks to the Liguna in bewilderment, "But of course," Kaliska cheers and claps her hands as the Murin insists, "We *must* study these creatures. There is so little known of them, any firsthand knowledge would be invaluable to us and possibly to the collective knowledge of the whole of Arsalia, perhaps even the world!"

Danahlia shakes her head stubbornly and then

points after the titan, "No freaking way. Who knows what that thing might do if it spotted you, or any of us."

"This is precisely why we are obligated to learn, to gather knowledge so that we and others may benefit," argues Twinkaleni.

Before things can escalate further, Alice offers to the Murin, "Why don't we go look for the elemental and study him?" Then to Danahlia she says, "It's way smaller *and* if it gets nasty, the caves are too small for it to pass through so we can run away." Squiggles burps loudly after finishing his meal, a hot smelly thing that prompts Alice to add, "Plus, we have Squigs."

Agreeing to this, the girls head back through the steam bellowing caves. The trip through the mountain is long but the girls do not lose their way. With their passage lit mostly by Twinkaleni's magic, the party follows the many scratch marks Squiggles had left in the cave's walls and floor with his claws as he investigated rock formations for mineral content, and they guess flavor. Soon, they reemerge on the other side, back in Arsalia, if a remote part of it. They find the elemental's cave from before when they came with Weiya, a young member of the Cloudstalkers, the tribe of Wakuwai the girls had befriended and spent much of the past winter with.

This cave isn't quite large enough to fit Squiggles but that doesn't stop him from trying to follow after the girls. When he finds he can go no further, he begins to scratch and dig out the sides of the cave with his incredibly durable claws. It's dirty, dusty work and the girls must wait outside while Squiggles enlarges the passage, appearing eager, perhaps even drawn, to get deeper. Twinkaleni suggests this may be due to the ambient energy emanating from the cave and possibly the elemental itself. This energy is felt by both Kaliska and Twinkaleni but remains a mystery to Alice and Danahlia, neither being gifted with magic.

Squiggles does remarkably well with his digging, his sharp claws ripping through softer rock and earth with ease while his hind legs shoveling back the debris, but it still takes time and eventually the dragon must rest. He emerges from the cave walking backwards, waving his long tail to insure nothing is behind him. His deep red scales have mostly become pale gray from all the dust but he seems happy, if exhausted, from his work. After he has some water, he curls up and lies down for a nap. Just this one drink has drained a significant portion of the girl's water supply, so they decide it best to look for a source.

As they do, Twinkaleni offers what little else she knows of titans. It's fairly common knowledge that the titans had once ruled all the land. With their incredible size, strength, and longevity, the earthen behemoths went unchallenged in the world for many ages, until people learned to tame dragons. Once great in number, dragons were one of few beings that could stand even a slim chance against the titans. Their own size and strength, while considerable, was still as nothing to the living mountains. Their true power lay in their flight and fire. On the backs of their fierce mounts, early dragon riders used their dragon's breath to defeat the titans and raise kingdoms on the lands claimed from the stone giants. Over time, the eastern kingdoms slowly merged into what is presently known as Arsalia.

Less known by most is that before the titans, there were other civilizations, possibly greater than those that exist today. These were empires given form by sorcerers, wielders of magic more powerful than any that have come since. Tapping into ancient sources of primal energies, these highly skilled mages used great spells to maintain absolute order and control in their realms. Twinkaleni admits she does not know why and can only speculate further, but at some point in history, these sorcerers fell from power. Without their magical might and leadership, their early empires crumbled, beginning what the small Murin calls a *dark age.* During this time, all the grand achievements of these ancient civilizations were lost, giving rise to chaos, fear, instability, and conflict. This was known as the Age of Titans.

She suspects that those very ancient sorcerers may have had something to do with the titans but has trouble imagining the sheer magnitude of magical energies needed to control, much less create, such creatures.

Twinkaleni is prattling on as she generally does when something interests her, "As far as I can figure, only a sizable rift would provide the necessary energy to manage such a feat but even then-"

"Hey, there's some," Danahlia interrupts, nodding to a fast running stream. The girls were gratefully finding these to be a fairly common sight in the mountains. As winter gave way to spring, former snow ladened peaks were giving birth to many new streams and swelling older waterways. As the girls are refilling their various receptacles with the ice cold water, Alice wonders what Twinkaleni plans to do with the elemental, should they find it again.

"I would very much like to study it, uncover its purpose, its reason for existing, find out how it came to be if possible," says Twinkaleni.

"You think we can be friends with it?" wonders Kaliska, capping one of her waterskins.

"I highly doubt that will be a possibility. Elementals are simply elements animated by magic, similarly to how I can animate water. Pavata!" Twinkaleni thrusts her tiny bare pink hands before her up stream and raises them slowly. As she does the stream's water lifts almost like one picking up part of a long ribbon. The water behind the held batch spills around it, wetting and chilling the girls' feet.

"Hey!" Danahlia complains pattering away to

dry land with Alice and Kaliska. Twinkaleni remains dry, the spilling water parting around her while she manipulates the held portion of the stream some to show her control over it.

"But if you're controllin' the water, what was controllin' the elemental?" Alice asks.

Twinkaleni releases the stream with a drop of her hands, "*That* is precisely what I would like to find out."

The girls find Squiggles right where they left him napping and decide to enter the cave. It doesn't take them long to find the end of it blocked by a large stone.

Placing a hand on the obstruction, Alice offers, "Maybe it caved in."

Disappointed, Twinkaleni gives the stone a few pushes with her tiny hand, the other holding a magical light, "Most unfortunate. It may be some time be-"

The stone moves.

"Whoa!" Danahlia cries and the girls immediately back away, the large, heavy stone sliding noisily to the side.

Smaller rocks are shaken loose around them, tumbling from the ceiling and walls, kicking up dust. Stone pops and grinds on the other side of the wall as the girls continue backing away. Almost the moment the stone finishes sliding off to the side, a slab like appendage is thrust into the girl's tunnel. They shriek and backpedal, the slab crashing into the wall of the tunnel with such force that the entire cave shakes, more rocks and dust falling atop them.

"It's the elemental!" shouts Twinkaleni, backing into Alice's legs.

"It's cranky!" calls Kaliska over the loud rumble and crack of sliding stone.

The sound quiets as the girls regain their balance, alertly watching the slab for any movement.

After a few moments of near silence, Alice asks, "Think it's stuck?"

As if to answer her, a deafening crash reverberates through the earth to their side. They're nearly taken from their feet from the impact, the shockwave causing larger rocks to shake loose from the ceiling, some dropping painfully on their heads.

"We need to get outta here!" yells Danahlia, already heading back the way they'd come.

The girls hold their arms out to the walls, trying to maintain balance while making a hasty retreat. The impact noise has stopped but the cave continues to rumble, its stability failing. Worried cries of alarm sound from her friends as Alice tries to keep pace with the Liguna, feeling Twinkaleni and Kaliska right behind her. As the rumbling continues, rocks fall in their path needing to be avoided as they make their way toward the light ahead. Then suddenly, the light is gone.
Alice thinks the cave must have collapsed trapping them but then hears Squiggles calling for them, his body blocking the cave as he sticks his head in to investigate.

"Squigs! Move! Back!" Danahlia shouts reaching the dragon and pushing on his muzzle. Squiggles complains as the others amass around his head, shouting and pushing to get him to back out of the way. Eventually, he figures out what they want and crawls backwards, letting the girls flee the collapsing tunnel. Once more in the open air, they cough dust from their throats and shake debris from their fur.

"Is everyone ok?" asks Alice, brushing dust from her ears. Fortunately, aside from a few scrapes and bruises, everyone is fine.

Waiting her turn to be healed by Kaliska, Danahlia looks back to the dust and steam pluming cave, "Well, at least it didn't completely-" as she speaks the cave rumbles once more and the ceiling collapses, blocking the tunnel and forcing the girls to move further away to avoid the resulting dust cloud, "Never mind."

Squiggles half opens his wings and grumbles, disappointed to see all his digging go to waste. He nuzzles around at the debris while the girls discuss what to do next. Squiggles begins to dig again, shoveling back loose rocks with his feet. The party decides to stick around as they had planned, mostly on Twinkaleni's insistence. They still have food with them and the growing abundance of the mountain forest for when that ran out. Then with a stream nearby, all they really needed was shelter.

After a bit of exploring, they manage to find another cave among the dozen or so that has also collapsed at some point, keeping its odorous steam trapped behind a wall of rock and stone. While not being very large or deep, it does give the girls a place to store some supplies as well as a dry place to sleep. Squiggles continues his efforts to dig out the elemental's tunnel while the four girls prepare their new camp site.

Due to the cave's size, the girls figure they will have to perform most activities just outside. The first thing they do is clear out the cave some, removing rocks and other debris so they can place their things inside along with a few skins to lie on. With the rocks, they set up a fire pit and Danahlia begins what she wants to become a wall around the camp. The others clear the area outside the cave some while discussing further improvement. Squiggles eventually comes to find them and they're able to use the growing dragon, now larger than most horses and considerably so if one counted his long neck and tail, to haul away some of the heavier stones. Danahlia has to fend off the dragon occasionally, who thinks her wall is something for him to snack on.

The party spends a few days at their camp, sometimes exploring, sometimes foraging, and other times hunting. Squiggles is determined to dig out the cave he was widening and is often at it for hours a day, resting and eating only to resume his work. The girls speculate as to why but at this point they really don't know what drives the great reptile. If his past behavior is any indicator, it is likely just because he thinks he'll find something good to eat.

The girls check on the dragon's work day by day, seeing him get deeper and deeper in until only his rump sticks out, then only his tail, and eventually his entire body can disappear into the tunnel. It's about this time that the girls are taking a break. While they watch the dragon's progress, mostly just dust flowing out with the rotten egg smelling steam, they hear the low rumble of earth shifting about. Alice immediately bolts to the cave, fearing another collapse and calls to Squiggles from the cave mouth. She's quickly joined by her friends, worriedly looking into the dark, steamy tunnel, encouraging the dragon to return.

The rumbling within continues and bits of rock tumble as even more dust bellows forth. Squiggles roars from within, more in surprise than anger. The girls call to him more urgently as the rumbling gets louder and the cave becomes less stable. Eventually, they see the dragon's tail whipping behind him to make sure his path is clear as he crawls slowly backward out of the cave. Once Squiggles' head pulls away from the cave mouth, they see he is staring very intently down the tunnel. The rumbling gets louder and more intense, prompting everyone to back away as even large stones, well above the cave, begin to shake loose and tumble down.

The girls decide to retreat to the safety of the nearby trees, though Squiggles only backs off a little. They call to him but he refuses to budge any further, glaring into the depths of the cave.

"What's happening?!" asks Kaliska, practically shouting over the rumble of earth and tumbling stone.

"It is likely the elemental! It was probably buried in the last cave in and is undoubtedly trying to get free!" says Twinkaleni, "This will be," she pauses to use a tree as cover from a rolling stone,

"This will be an excellent opportunity to see how an elemental reacts to a dragon.

"You want 'em to fight?!" asks Alice, looking down at the Murin beside her, a tree trunk at her back.

"Nothin' gonna stop that now! Look!" Danahlia points from around her own tree.

Squiggles pulls back his head and steadily opens his wings as the cave continues to rumble. The side of the cave, open to the air, bursts with the deafening crash of thick, solid stone smashing through its lesser formed ilk. A length of stone Alice though was part of the cave wall, lingers in midair, revealing itself to be an appendage of some kind. Almost like the segments of a scorpion's tail, the appendage is made up of large slabs of monolithic stones linked by unknown means. Once free, it immediately curls on itself, slamming its broad end into the mountain side it protrudes from like a sledgehammer. The force of the strike thunders with such terrifying power that the girls can only cower and hold down their ears.

After another earth shattering blow, Alice

hears Squiggles roar his challenge. She peeks around her tree to see the dragon closing on the massive stone appendage, his wings spread wide. Not sure if it would help but not wanting to see the dragon get any closer to the elemental, Alice screams, "INFERMIOUS!"

Whether because of Alice's command or because it was in the dragon's strategy, Squiggles roars fiercely once more, a wide cone of bright yellow and orange flame pouring out with it. The blaze floods over the end of the stone giant's limb as it uncurls for another strike. Somehow the stone catches. Squiggles' flame turns to an emerald inferno as it wraps around the stone segments. The strange fire is particularly concentrated at the joints and burns fiercely as the limb manages one last mighty blow before simply falling off. But it's enough.

Even with its limb fallen limply away, still burning green, the cave was damaged sufficiently that the rest of the elemental is able to attempt to free its enormous body from its underground prison. Piles of rubble are sent flying into the air, forcing Squiggles back as more limbs break free of the earth's binding. One that curls downward seems to be a leg as another that joins it is a second swinging arm. These grip the mountain around it and pull with rock powdering force until a portion of crab like body is torn free, followed by a massive rectangular head.

Squiggles isn't interested in letting the creature emerge fully and charges back in with a flaming roar. As the inferno approaches, the elemental curls its freed arm around a large chunk of its fallen predecessor and hurls it with careless strength at the young dragon. Perhaps unable to see through his own fire, Squiggles is caught by surprise when the stone projectile clips one of his hind legs, sending him staggering to his side with a pained cry. The girls call his name in worry but see little they can do to help. The elemental uses the lull in battle to pull more of its massive asymmetrical form from the earth while freeing another segmented limb. Squiggles launches another blast of fire, but the flames barely reach the elemental, only singeing the end of a limb.

"Alice, you *must* guide Squiggles' efforts! Get him to launch another blast at the center of the elemental," shouts Twinkaleni.

"How?" asks Alice frantically looking from the Murin, to the elemental, and then to the hurt dragon.

"You *must!*" insists the small mage, "I will try to lend aid from here."

Not sure what she could do but fearing what might happen if she does nothing, Alice flings herself from the safety of her tree and dashes to Squiggles' side. Her first instinct is to check on his leg, which doesn't look broken but the stone has left some of his scales shattered and the flesh underneath in tatters. Squiggles sees her from the corner of his eye and brings a wing to wrap over her protectively. While she looks over his wounded leg wondering what to do, Squiggles' wing suddenly presses her against his body as he clamors to the side, only just avoiding another hurled stone slab from the elemental. This shows Alice how greatly hampered the dragon's movements are, but it also gives her an idea.

Squiggles is forced low from the sudden shift and Alice is able to climb a front limb, shouting, "Squigs, you have ta fly!"

An unconfident flier at best, especially when taking off from the ground, Squiggles makes a distressed noise. Alice uses the dragon's tough scales as handholds to climb atop his back and sit on the base of his neck just before his wings.

She calls encouragingly, patting the dragon, "Come on boy, you can do it!"

The dragon makes an deep apprehensive drumming in his throat and begins to flap his wings. Alice had only ridden on Squiggles lightly a few times and only while he walked. Not even Twinkaleni had ridden him yet as he flew. The elemental pulls the rest of its strangely shaped form from the remains of the cave, curling a limb around another large chunk of its dismembered arm. Alice hears her friends calling her name fearfully as she encourages the dragon upward, holding tight to his neck as she bobs up and down with his flapping.

The elemental looses the stone missile at them as they hear Danahlia scream, "LOOK OUT!"

With all the strength his legs can muster, Squiggles leaps, Alice nearly falling off his side from the move. The stone crashes into the earth the dragon had just occupied, fragmenting with the impact. Pebbles fly up at Alice as she scrambles to regain her seating while Squiggles roars his success, flapping frantically to keep gravity from bringing him back down. Now aloft, Squiggles, weather by design or not, has hovered closer to the elemental, enough that it attempts to swipe one of its long, segmented appendages at him. Squiggles leans back to avoid it and Alice can feel the air wave generated by the massive stone slabs as they pass alarmingly near, only to crash deafeningly into the side of the mountain.

Thin streams of fire begin to run over the elemental at various points as it recovers, Twinkaleni attempting to damage or distract the earthen creature with her magic. Alice must hold on tight as the elemental tries to backhand them. Squiggles drifts and bobs awkwardly in the air as he attempts to keep from the monster's long reach, now almost directly over it.

Alice sees the attack has left the elemental's torso exposed and as Squiggles tries desperately to right himself, she shouts, pointing, "Squigs, infermious!"

Unable to see the fox girl's direction but understanding the command, Squiggles unleashes a bellowing roar with a river of fire. Losing focus on his flapping, Squiggles' altitude drops with the blast but scores a direct hit. As his fiery breath pours down on the elemental, the creature is consumed by the same strange, green fire from before. The earth creature does not cry out or make any other noise of discomfort other than the crackling pop of stone. After coating the elemental's body in flame, Squiggles tries to climb once more. But before he can ascend even a few feet, another of the elemental's limbs comes swiftly for him.

The arm begins to collapse, it's joints eroding under the heat of the emerald flame, but the large, fist like end segment has built enough momentum to stay on course. The dragon is unable to maneuver out of the way this time and Alice watches in panicked horror as the stone slab flies to claim her.

From below, Twinkaleni screams, "GRAVITUS!"

The encroaching stone veers off slightly at a downward angle coming so close that one of Squiggles' tucked fore claws scratches it's surface as it sails just under them. Alice turns to see the slab crash through tree and brush, leaving a sizable whole in the mountain forest's thick foliage. Excited by the elemental's weakened state, Squiggles lets himself drop atop it, letting loose with more of his dragon fire, bathing in flame any part of the creature still moving. The elemental collapses with a thunderous crash under the weight of the dragon and his fire. The emerald flames that engulfs the fallen earth monster's body don't seem to bother the dragon in the least as he glares, daring it to move. Alice, however, is very much aware of the heat radiating from below and tucks her body close atop the dragon as she clings to his neck.

Squiggles turns to the sky and erupts with a thunderous triumphant roar as if to announce his victory across the entirety of the Gadara Mountain range. Once the flames die down and Squiggles is sure the elemental will not rise again, he crawls off the creature's ruined body and let's Alice slide off to the whooping and cheering of Danahlia.

The lizard girl grabs Alice up in a hug, squeezing tight, "Ticks! You did it! How'd you-" Squiggles whips his head around to hiss angrily at Kaliska, poking about his injured leg.

The deer girl puts up her hands in surrender, "Ok, ok, but it is hurt pretty bad."

"Can you do anything for 'im?" Alice asks.

"I can try," says Kaliska, clapping her hands under Squiggles watchful gaze.

Alice spots Twinkaleni breathing hard, and exclaims, "You saved us."

Twinkaleni waves a negligent hand, still trying to catch her breath and Alice pulls free of Danahlia's grasp to kneel beside the Murin, giving her a hug.

"Yeah, not bad, Mini Mage," Danahlia says approvingly, using a hand to ruffle the light gray fur atop the mouse girl's head.

Twinkaleni smacks the hand away, huffing, "A minor, effort."

Danahlia grins and looks over the heaps of stone and rock that was the cave and elemental, the green fire having died off, "So, how we gonna explain this to the Cloudstalkers?"

Chapter 2

Home

Kaliska finds that she can't heal Squiggles' leg very well. Twinkaleni suggests his own natural magic resistance is likely the reason and the girls decide to stay at their cave campsite until the young dragon can recover. During this time, Alice and Danahlia hunt while remaining on the look out for herbs and plants Kaliska thinks may help speed Squiggles' recovery. Twinkaleni stays by the caves with the dragon, greatly interested in the stones left behind by the elemental's demise.

She says even though Squiggles' fire had burned away much of the stones' animating magical energy, some still remained. For the most part, the stones looked like any other, though in the darkest night the faintest green glow can be seen emanating from a few of them. These are mostly the portions that made up the elemental's torso. Squiggles is interested in these too and claws at one in particular while he rests. He eats the bits of stone he scratches off while Twinkaleni will occasionally swipe one for her own study.

After a successful hunting trip, Alice and Danahlia arrive in camp to find Twinkaleni fleeing from Squiggles, the dragon limping after her with annoyed grumbles. The small mouse girl trips over some rubble and a large, black object is sent tumbling from her grasp. The dragon immediately goes for this as Twinkaleni scrambles to crawl over it, curling her body around the object protectively while the dragon looms over her, frustrated.

"No! You can't have it!" cries Twinkaleni, shooing the dragon away with one tiny pink hand.

Squiggles nudges her with his muzzle, trying to get the Murin to roll over and relinquish the thing he covets. He manages easily but Twinkaleni stubbornly rolls herself more, keeping her back to him.

"Uh, what are you doin'?" asks Danahlia.

Twinkaleni looks over her shoulder at the returned pair, demanding, "Bring this beast to heel! He can't have it!"

As if to make his own protest, Squiggles turns

his head to Alice and Danahlia making a throaty whine. Alice draws the dragon away by offering him one of the thickly maned rabbit like creatures she'd shot that morning. Squiggles crunches on the morsel, not minding the fur or bones in the least, and then tries for the others she holds. Alice laughs as he attempts to get his long, slobbery tongue around one and tosses a second maned hare away for the dragon to chase. While he lumbers off, Danahlia helps up the Murin, the mouse mage unable to use her arms as she refuses to release the object she's hoarding.

"What's that?" Alice wonders at the dark stone in the small girl's hands.

Twinkaleni considers before revealing the item in question, "This, I believe, is the stone around which the elemental had formed. It has the highest concentration of energy and was taken from its very center."

The stone is solid black and glitters like water in the sun. It's about two of Alice's fists in size, has rough and smooth faces, along with an asymmetrical shape. But what's more interesting is it's green glow, visible even in the light of day.

Danahlia reaches for the stone but Twinkaleni pulls it away.

"Ticks, Twinkie, I'm not gonna take it. I just wanna see," Danahlia complains.

Twinkaleni grudgingly lets her hold the glowing rock. Alice has it next. Other than the glow and feeling heavy for its size, the stone seems fairly ordinary.

"Squigs wanted this?" Alice asks, holding out the stone.

Twinkaleni takes it back, keeping it close. "Indeed. I believe he planned to eat it," she says with a distasteful look to the dragon, approaching once more. Twinkaleni scampers away with her treasure before he can get any closer. Squiggles, uninterested in giving chase, nudges Alice's shoulder with his muzzle.

Alice turns from him to protect her two remaining rabbits, saying good-naturedly, "No Squigs, these are for us. You had plenty."

In imitation of her speech, Squiggles complains

with a few whiny grumbles. Alice stays firm, smiling to herself. Rejected, Squiggles limps away to plop heavily down atop the remaining chunks of elemental to rest.

As days pass, Kaliska's continued herbal ministrations see Squiggles' leg healed fully while Twinkaleni continues her studies of the mysterious rock the girls come to call, the stone heart. The small mage says the stone heart is similar to the core stones found within the jelly monsters in the pixie forest near Alice's hometown of Toki. She goes on to say that the magic contained within the core stones was highly complex, intricate and purposeful. She is confident now, after studying the stone heart, that the jellies were created by some forgotten mage's hand for yet unknown purpose. The stone heart on the other hand, she claims, was transmuted by natural means.

From what the mage feels from the stone's energies, she concludes it was created very slowly over a great period of time, with only bits of will added by ambient magic over possibly many centuries. When asked whose will could have infused it so, she says she does not know, but judging from the elemental's shape, it may have been the various denizens of the mountain's many caves. These being mostly mere insects, Twinkaleni suggests that over time, the collective will of all these creatures, over many generations, may have steadily shaped the elemental's form and behavior, with the help of whatever abundant magic still remained hidden within the mountains.

Eager to unlock the mountains' secrets, Twinkaleni encourages Squiggles to resume digging into the elemental's cave. Apparently without fear of further engagement with the earth and magic born creatures, Squiggles does so with fervor. Twinkaleni remains by the caves, occasionally using her magic to clear boulders and other debris. Kaliska takes to foraging for edible plants and medicinal herbs nearby, allowing Alice and Danahlia to wander off on hunting expeditions. The pair do hunt much of the time, but going on these trips has become more about being together. Alice finds her affection for the Liguna continuing to grow, even to the point that she becomes excited at the idea of going on another outing whenever they aren't already on one.

Today's hunting trip starts like any other. After breakfast, the pair set off by bidding their friends a good day. Twinkaleni and Squiggles remain busily digging into the mountain while Kaliska randomly mixes various herbal concoctions with the intent of inventing some sort of salve, just in case Squiggles or the others are injured in the future. The moment Danahlia and Alice are out of view, they immediately begin their ritual of chasing each other through the mountain forest. A tug on the tail, Danahlia's having almost fully grown back, means the chased is now the chaser.

They run after each other with abandon, knowing dangers could lurk anywhere but far too absorbed in their games to pay it any mind. By the time they're both breathing hard, Alice gives Danahlia's tail a tug, only to have the Liguna surprise her with a tackle, taking them both to the ground. They roll through the new spring grasses laughing joyously until Danahlia ends up atop Alice. The fox girl's sky blue eyes meet the Liguna's green slitted ones. They smile at each other, Alice gingerly running a hand along Danahlia's waist and hip as the lizard girl caresses one of her furry cheeks. Danahlia leans in but let's Alice make the effort to reach up and kiss her lips. They've done this frequently in their seclusion but the warmth, the flutter, the tingle, remains strong and sought.

After taking the time to savor one another, Danahlia pulls away and gets a little lick on her nose. Grinning widely, the lizard girl pins Alice's arms and begins nuzzling the inside of her triangular ears. The fluff inside a Tokala's ears is especially sensitive and it tickles Alice terribly. She laughs and writhes, turning her head this way and that, but facing one ear to the ground exposes the other and Danahlia is swift to take advantage. Only after Alice is rendered breathless and near choking from laughter does Danahlia let up, rolling to her side in the grass beside the gasping fox girl.

The Liguna smiles as Alice tries to catch her breath, "Let's live here."

Alice, chest heaving, nods, "Ok." And they do.

For many months, the girls live peacefully in the mountains with their dragon. The spring season brings a bounty of food and the vast expanse of mountain forest begs to be explored. As they grow accustomed to the ways of the mountains, the girls steadily claim them as their home. Twinkaleni and Kaliska frequently remain by the cave side camp, the Murin studying the magical energies present in the earth there while Kaliska looks after her and makes the base more homey. Naturally curious, Alice tends to take Danahlia, and occasionally Squiggles, to roam all over the mountains in search of adventure.

The Cloudstalkers appear to have an invisible barrier around their winter campsite. No doubt built by their reputation as skilled hunters and fierce warriors, even larger ferals seem to respect it. But beyond this is a very wild world filled with many unusual creatures, not all friendly. Expeditions into these unknown regions, thus, often lead to many new things for the girls to see and experience.

Many ferals give birth in the spring. Sometimes, if they're quiet and more than a little lucky, they can see an infant with it's mother, or small herds with newborns among them. Kaliska seems to have a unique way with ferals. Many that would flee on sight or scent of the others, tend to only seem curious around the Chitali. Kaliska says it's because they know she doesn't plan to eat them, though Twinkaleni thinks it may have more to do with her aura, a sort of faint energy emitted by the magically gifted. Occasionally, Kaliska will lead her companions to injured ferals, claiming to be guided to them by her goddess, Althea. She then uses her healing magic to restore twisted limbs, bent wings, and other such injuries. Doing so affords the girls a chance to see many illusive creatures up close, if only briefly.

Another welcome discovery are what the girls decide to call, honey ants. Golden in color, these forearm length insects frequent a specific type of tree during the day. When they arrive, the large mandibled soldiers cut into the their favored tree's branches which causes sap to leak out. One of their caste consumes the sap, drinking so much that it's abdomen swells to the size of a melon. The tree's sap raw is rather bland and runny, but something the ants do to it turns the same sap into a much sought delicacy. By the afternoon, these ants can become so engorged on the sap that they can no longer move and must be carried back to their nests by groups of workers. The girls take to raiding these supply chains, dashing in and snatching up the most swollen ants before the soldiers and workers can react. Their reward for doing so is a sweet, viscous honey-like goo and a tasty ant.

During their time in the mountains, Squiggles steadily grows on wild game and his scales become shiny and hard with all the minerals he eats. He regularly lets the girls ride him now, even two or three at a time when he's in the mood, though with his interest in the cave's excavation, he rarely flies. After uncovering the cavern that originally housed the elemental, Squiggles makes it his own, frequently retiring within to rest and sleep. This chamber has many tunnels that in turn branch off to others. Some are large enough for Squiggles to wander through even if he chose to hold out his expansive wings, while others are too small even for Twinkaleni.

The steam within the larger tunnels tends to keep to the ceiling, making venturing through them far easier, though Twinkaleni feels all should be thoroughly searched. The Murin mage, very systematically, leads expeditions into the steam bellowing mountains' depths whenever she can get anyone to follow. When she isn't mapping out the tunnels, using a system of symbols she's devised for reference, she's studying the properties of the various rocks she finds. So invested in the caves has she become that she often sleeps within them with Squiggles, despite the constant stench of rotten eggs. On the increasingly rarer times she emerges and joins the others for a meal, she can't help but prattle on about her discoveries.

The magic contained in a great deal of the caves' rock, but mostly in the elemental, have the Murin mage revisiting the possibilities of enchanting. Twinkaleni had been interested in the fusion of magical energies into objects to give them special properties since back in the pixies' forest, where she had access to the jelly monsters' core stones. Though once they had left it behind, she had lost the opportunity to experiment. She says now that it was for the best, as the core stones were far too complex for her to practice with. The cave rock, however, she believes will be perfect for her renewed study.

She says that the stones that make up some of the deeper caves, and the elemental especially, share very similar aspects with enchanted items, though their far greater simplicity has inspired the small mage to perform various tests. She goes on in length while the others eat, explaining why she believes the core stones often exploded and what she is trying to manage with the cave rocks that is different. Alice finds it difficult to follow the Murin's rapidly spoken details but she imagines enchantment working somewhat like putting clothes into a pack.

When clothes are crammed thoughtlessly in, they are messy and the pack tends to fill faster. But, if one folds the clothes and places them neatly and carefully within, the pack can generally hold more and the clothes stay neat. Alice had seen Twinkaleni prove this plenty while carefully packing away her own belongings, but the fox girl, along with the others, preferred the simpler stuffing method. This concept seemed to relate to enchantment in a similar way. The core stones of jelly monsters were a very complex pack that needed to be filled with energy very carefully, otherwise they would become unstable and burst, or sometimes melt. The stones found in the caves however are much simpler, still requiring what Twinkaleni terms "folding magic," but requiring less careful placement of the energies that the mage could channel into them. After a time, Twinkaleni begins to excitedly shows her friends various pebbles she's managed to enchant.

Alice and Danahlia congratulate the Murin on her achievements, though handling the pebbles themselves reveals little distinguishing the small rocks from any others. Even so, Twinkaleni delights in explaining her process, claiming that she has taken the energies of one pebble and placed it into another, nearly doubling whatever intangible earth energies are contained in one while stripping the other. The mage says transferring energy from one like object into another is much simpler than trying to enchant an item from scratch, and says doing so is excellent practice. She claims that eventually, she may even gain the experience needed to recharge Jellybane, Alice's sword. Enchanted by pixies nearly a year ago, Jellybane had long been depleted of it's magical energies after extended use. The girls are glad the Murin has found something to occupy herself, especially since it doesn't involve her more dangerous magic.

Meanwhile, Alice and Danahlia collect quite a few skins on their hunts, which they scrape clean for various uses such as bedding and flooring. With what they've learned from the Cloudstalkers, they also manage to make other items as well. Knives and tools from bones and horns, pouches and packs from hides, and they even make a few necklaces adorned with teeth to display their hunting prowess. Clothes, however, prove to be a challenge for the girls.

The furs of beasts were wonderfully warm in the winter but in the growing heat of late spring, cooler garments to replace their well worn rags are needed. They try to craft clothes from what is available but lacking proper knowledge, what they come up with is of poor quality. Kaliska also has a persistent desire to wear something that wasn't "torn from helpless murdered creatures." Danahlia suggests everyone go bare furred, but with even the remote possibility of encountering someone, this doesn't get a tremendous amount of support.

Seeing little alternative, the girls prepare to head back to the Hollow, the home they'd made for themselves among the massive roots of an ancient zalonya tree. The Hollow, being larger than their cave side camp and closer to the foot of the Gadara mountains, is better suited for storage as well as their planned future trade ventures. Twinkaleni needs a great deal of coaxing before she will leave the caves. She feels her time would be better spent in continued study of the magic within the mountains, but being only thirteen and very small, even for a Murin, the others refuse to leave her alone. Once Squiggles is ladened with many of the girl's things, he is also forced to carry a load of rocks Twinkaleni insist on having so she might continue her precious work at their main camp. Even with Squiggles carrying most of the magic infused stones,

Twinkaleni keeps the stone heart to herself, very seldom parting with it, even when sleeping.

The walk to the Hollow is one of nearly a day, made longer with all the party carries. When they arrive, they are relieved and rest for a time. They clean their home some and further discuss their plans for trading with the small settlements that dot the region just south of the Gadara Mountains. They know little of the land save for what they saw on their way through it and decide it will be best to check one they know of first. Collecting their finest skins and various other items they feel will be valued for barter, the girls head south.

Approaching the edge of their mountain forest home, Alice, Kaliska, and Twinkaleni take their trade goods, leaving Danahlia to look after Squiggles until they return. Another day's walk sees them to a small farming community were they manage to barter for clothes, vegetables, and a few small things, but most importantly, they gather information about other nearby settlements. The trio do not manage to come across a map, but are told of a few more spots they might seek trade with in the future. With the success of their trade mission, the girls return to the mountains.

On their way back, Twinkaleni pulls free a small pendant of sorts. She's made it from woven grass and a piece of one of Squiggles' scales, broken off in his battle with the elemental, tied to one end. Alice watches as the Murin lets it hang and then channels her energy into the object, causing the scale end to lift as if by some slight breeze Alice cannot feel. The scale leads them directly back to where Danahlia and Squiggles await their companions in the safety of the trees. After warm greetings, the girls make their way back to the Hollow. Twinkaleni is eager to get back to the caves and Squiggles decides he wants to follow. Kaliska joins them so she may look after the small Murin. This leaves Alice and Danahlia, who choose to stay saying they want to see what game spring has brought locally.

There friends a ways off now, Alice and Danahlia have ample opportunity to truly enjoy one another. After the difficulty of winter, the pair had hunted a fair bit and can live comfortably on their stores for a time. They continue to hunt when the need or desire for fresh meat presents itself, but for now, they relax. Danahlia has found a large flat rock on which the pair have taken to lounging upon. Atop a layer of furs, they take in each new day lazily lying together. Danahlia likes to nap in the sun, curled around Alice. The Tokala, however, is eager for adventure and often finds it difficult to be patient. She takes to amusing herself by running her furred hands and legs over and under Danahlia's smooth ones, her muzzle nuzzling the Liguna's neck to pleased moans. Danahlia will hold her a bit tighter, rolling more of her weight onto the slim fox girl to keep her from moving so much as she tries to doze.

This only makes Alice squirm more, prompting Danahlia to take hold of her hands and wrap strong legs around her own, squeezing Alice. Left with few options, the Tokala will then rub her nose about the Liguna's chin and lips, licking her periodically, while still squirming. Eventually, Danahlia will give up on napping, trying to mask laughter with irritation, saying something akin to "Ok, ok, I'm up. Let's go do somethin'." Then Alice will cheer and run off to gather their things.

Their days are spent exploring the vast and wild mountains, making note of their discoveries, food in the form of edible flora or fauna, water sources, new creatures, and other points of interest. When Alice's curiosity is sated, they return to the

Hollow, spending nights curled under blankets together. As Danahlia holds her in her arms, gently stroking her fur while resting her chin atop the fox girl's head, their legs intertwined, Alice sighs, contentedly thinking if this is how the rest of her life is to be spent, she wouldn't mind at all.

Chapter 3

Changes

Over the next few months, the girls venture between the Hollow and the caves frequently. Twinkaleni and Kaliska will often ride Squiggles down to take part in trade expeditions. The Murin is in constant need of paper and, more importantly, empty journals to write about her many discoveries and experiments within the mountains. This means she is perpetually pestering Alice and Danahlia about acquiring more trade goods in the form of skins and meats so they may acquire some for her. Bringing down ferals for such purposes is a simple matter for the magically gifted mouse girl, who has devised an almost frighteningly simple way of dispatching them, even larger ones now, with her magic.

The way she has explained it is that her skill with water manipulation has grown to the point that she can now hold sway over the flow of blood in living creatures, causing it to collect and rupture parts of her target's brain. Ferals will often collapse, instantly dead when made victim of the spell. Alice and Danahlia insist their hunting is enough and that she doesn't need to use such magic, but the many processes needed to turn wild beasts into clean skins and dried meats takes time, time in which Twinkaleni's patients grows weaker while her interest in the mountain's secrets grows stronger.

Sometimes, the Murin will pull herself away from her studies to take Squiggles around the thick mountain forest, slaying animals with abandon, only to drop off a pile of corpses for Alice and Danahlia to prepare. She keeps from rushing them, only saying she wishes to increase efficiency by removing the girls' need to hunt. Squiggles seems to enjoy these trips as he gets plenty to eat. The Murin is also adept at drying meat with her magic, able to pull free the moisture from flesh far faster than any natural drying method. When they have enough of a load to take to market, the girls will ride Squiggles, who is growing ever larger and stronger on the mountain's bounty. Squiggles is left at the edge of the forest to keep from being seen, leaving the girls to walk, often great distances with heavy packs, to reach settlements.

This is greatly alleviated once Squiggles is strong enough to fly while carrying two girls, usually

Alice and Twinkaleni, on his back along with their trade goods. They only take to the sky at night and even then keep to clouds when they can to avoid notice. When they can't, Twinkaleni collects the moon and star light glimmering off the dragon's scales, and tucks them into a bright, little ball which she conceals in her pocket. This makes Squiggles look like a swiftly flying patch of black regardless of how bright the moon shines. They can only reach certain settlements in this manner, only those that have isolated bits of forest nearby so Squiggles can stay hidden while the girls move into town under cover of darkness. The dragon has learned to wait patiently until their return, knowing he will be rewarded for his good behavior.

After many ventures, the girls begin to map out the region along with the towns and villages there in. They learn who they can reliably sell their wares to and who to buy from but try to remain as low profile as possible. They will only visit settlements in an order that allows for time enough to pass between each visit in the hopes that any lingering memory of their passing will be vague or forgotten before they come again. They acquire simple cloaks and make there way in and out of town as discretely as they can, though some contacts are unavoidable.

Paper and, more so, journals, are rare items that not many smaller traders bother keeping in stock. Thus, many of their excursions are fruitless as far as Twinkaleni is concerned, but Alice enjoys bartering for decent deals and the perks of doing so. When they can't find what they're looking for, the girls often trade for other items, not wanting to lug the same meats and skins back with them. Freshly baked breads, clothing that actually fits, and fruit juices, are some of Alice's favorite finds when she is in the position to splurge a little. She also tries to look for things Danahlia might like, plus she must always bring back something for Squiggles.

Even so, she can't help seeing some familiar sights. People begging in the streets, sometimes a mother and child, or worse, a child alone. These especially give the fox girl pause, remembering her own time on the streets of Toki village, having no options but to beg and hope pity would be enough to see her through another day. Alice can never help herself when she sees children in need and rushes in her trades to get food for them. Sometimes she manages, sometimes their gone before she can come back, though the warmth in her heart at the slight aid she can offer is always worth the effort.

On one trading trip, Alice is accompanied by Kaliska, though the Chitali vanishes, as she often does, once they're in the settlement, claiming she is being led by Althea. This leaves Alice to do all the bargaining. As she is receiving a loaf of bread fresh from a baker selling his wares from a stall before a cleverly made portable oven, something small and dark, darts in and yanks at the loaf.

Instinctively, Alice tightens her grip, allowing an all black Feladine girl to tear free only a handful of bread before she flees around the corner, leaving Alice and the baker shouting, "Hey!"

"Dah, sorry miss. Little'uns been a problem for us all. Here lemme-" before the baker can finish, Alice tosses a few coins on his counter and dashes after the cat girl, calling back for the baker not to worry about it.

Alice rounds the corner, tucking her bread in close so she can pump her arms for more speed. The Feladine is swift and only offers a glimpse of her tail before disappearing again around a corner or down an alley. Several times Alice can only guess as to were she might have gone but is determined to catch up.

She enters a section of town on the outskirts that looks to have burnt down at some point. No one spared the effort to clean it up. Charred support beams and walls lay littered about with bits of foundation poking up through ash and soot, giving her an idea of where houses once stood. The Tokala treads carefully, having lost sight of the cat girl. She can smell her though, the faint wisp of fresh bread cutting through the dank scent of moldy, burnt wood. As she ventures further down a silent avenue, seemingly forgotten by the rest of the town, Alice can make out pawprints in the ash. She follows these silently, not wanting to scare the girl into running off again if she could help it.

The trail of prints eventually leads to a burnt out shack, still standing but appearing as if a good breeze could topple it. Entering what was left of a doorway, Alice notices the inside seems to have been cleaned some, blackened bits of wood having been swept off to the side and into corners. Alice follows small sooty paws into a room that looks to have been spared the worst of whatever fire had ravaged the neighborhood. Near the back wall of the room, squatting over a bundle of cloth, is the cat girl. Her back is to Alice, modest triangular ears focused on what lies on the floor before her. Perhaps eight or nine years of age, she wears the rags of what might have been a dress once, now filthy and torn, with her long ebony tail flicking in the air behind her.

She turns from the bundle to reach for a bowl of water. When she does, she spots Alice in her periphery and jumps, swiftly rising to her feet, hissing, while baring small fangs and short curved claws extending from now crooked fingers.

Alice holds out her bread in one hand and shows the palm of the other, "It's ok. I'm not gonna hurt you."

The cat girl hisses more menacingly, hunching over, her fur bristling. Alice slowly crouches, planning to place the bread on the floor and leave, but then the cloth bundle coughs pitifully. The Feladine almost turns back to it but decides to keep her eyes on Alice, showing more sharp teeth and raising a paw threateningly.

"I'm sorry. I didn't mean to frighten you. I just

wanted to give you this," says Alice, holding out her loaf of bread.

The Feladine bobs a little, claws and fangs still bared, as if wanting to do several things at once but not being able to decide on any. The bundle she protects coughs a bit more raggedly, the tiny handful of bread the girl had snatched rolling away from it. Alice can see that it's another child, this one even younger, wrapped in torn bits of clothing. A near infant Leeseran.

Alice continues to hold out the bread, speaking with much concern, "Your friend sounds sick. I know someone who can help. She's a healer and ca-"

The moment Alice's eyes are off of her, the cat girl flashes forward, snatching the bread and slashing at the air between her and Alice as if to ensure the Tokala doesn't follow. By the time Alice blinks, the girl is squatting on the other side of the squirrel pup, taking up the bowl of water to let her charge drink. She looks rapidly between the tiny child and Alice as he sips and returns his small bit of bread to him when he finishes. Once he has it, the Feladine glares back at Alice.

Alice nods, "Ok, I'll go get 'er, you just stay right here, ok?" The cat girl only glares back and Alice races off to find Kaliska.

Hurrying to their designated meeting spot and hoping the Chitali hadn't wandered off as she had developed a habit of doing, Alice is surprised to hear her name being called from a small house. The deer girl bursts from the doorway and bounds toward her calling, "Alice!"

Alice turns to her, "Kali! They're some kids who need-"

"I know, I know, let's go, let's go, let's go!" says Kaliska, flying by the Tokala, a family of Rotans calling their thanks after her from the dwelling she flew from.

The Chitali bounds down the wrong way in the street and Alice must guide her back in the direction of the children. Kaliska has said that her goddess, Althea, let's her feel people in distress. A very devoted healer by nature, this causes the Chitali to run off frequently and get lost, especially in larger settlements where she says people in need reach out to her from too many places at once. Keeping

Kaliska on track, Alice gets them back to the ruined shack to find the two children gone.

The pair search around and find a fresh trail of sooty footprints intermittently marked by bread crumbs. They follow it around through several burnt out buildings before it begins to head back toward the more lively part of town. As the prints become less defined, Alice hears angry words and hissing. Rounding a corner, the searching pair spot a group of older children, all in rags, and the Feladine girl struggling to hold onto the Leeseran as she's shoved to the ground by one of the others.

"Hey!" Alice shouts, charging at the group of four, possibly just coming into their teen years.

Alice had left her sword with Squiggles, not wanting it to make her stand out, but she did however have a concealed bone bladed knife. She doesn't need it though. The four look to her, one holding the loaf of bread she had given the cat girl, before fleeing the scene.

Alice gives them chase for a block or two, driven by the guilt of having made the girl a target with what she had thought was generosity. The children split up and are eventually lost to back alleys forcing the Tokala to give up. On her way back, she is left thinking of how foolish it was to give chase in the first place. What would she do if she caught them? Demand they go hungry so the girl and the tiny squirrel child wouldn't?

Alice retraces her hastily taken steps to find Kaliska looking over the Leeseran in the cat girl's arms. The young Feladine glares at her as she approaches, mistrust and perhaps some blame in her eyes.

"I'm sorry. I didn't mean for that to happen. I just wanted to help," says Alice sincerely. The girl's gaze doesn't lighten, broken only by a cough. Alice asks Kaliska, "How are they?"

The Chitali is passing her hands over the Leeseran and says glumly, "Hungry, dirty, and sick."

"Can you heal them?" Alice asks, getting her first good look at the squirrel pup. It's a boy, maybe a year old if that and obviously malnourished. His predominately brown and tan fur is peppered with a dash of gray and clings tightly to his fragile frame.

Kaliska massages the child's chest some through the rags that cover him, "Maybe, but it'll take a while. It's in his lungs. We need to take 'em home. I have some herbs that should help."

"Take 'em, home?" Alice wonders, looking over the children. This seemed like a tremendous leap from offering some food but it did sound like the right thing to do, though Alice considers if she and her friends are up for such responsibility.

"Yup yup," chimes Kaliska, then to the cat girl says, "You should come with us, we have food, and a tree house, and we can sing, AND we have the cutest little Murin!" Kaliska goes on listing all the things the girls and their mountain home have to offer.

The Feladine looks confused, as if a part of her wants to just run away while the other wants to hear more. Alice gives her an encouraging smile, remembering her own humble youth and wondering what it must be like to be offered so much after having so little.

"How about we get somethin' to eat first?" offers Alice, feeling the few coins she has left in one pocket.

"I *am* hungry," Kaliska announces, "Come on, it'll be fun, let's go!" The Chitali takes choice from the silent Feladine, plucking the Leeseran from her arms and heading back toward the market. The cat girl follows with Alice behind her.

Alice purchases some more bread with the money that was suppose to go to Squiggle's treat for waiting patiently in the woods. He would have to understand. She hands one of the two loaves to Kaliska, who shares with the tiny squirrel boy, and then breaks hers in half, holding it out to the Feladine. The girl pauses warily.

"It's ok. No ones gonna take it from you, not unless they get through us," Alice assures, though Kaliska doesn't make the most steadfast companion, talking gibberish to the Leeseran in her arms as she feeds him crumbs.

The Feladine sticks up her lower lip and takes the bread, holding it before her as if uncertain as to what to do with it. After a moment, she pulls the bread in close and looks back to Alice, her eyes watery but refusing to cry. Instead she just sniffles wetly and follows along.

Leaving town and heading for where they left their dragon, Alice and Kaliska tell the Feladine all about where they intend to take her and the infant squirrel boy she had been caring for. Once she finished her bread, she had taken the Leeseran back into her arms and now looks a little more comfortable, listening to the older girls. She has said nothing of herself, seemingly intent on ignoring all questions, even when asked her name. Still, the hours long walk is not silent as Kaliska goes on in length about all the wonderful things there will be to do when they bring their guests home.

"Ok, don't be afraid. He's big but he won't hurt you," assures Alice as they approach where Squiggles waits.

The dragon makes his usual greeting grumble as they near and lumbers over to them, squishing bushes and pushing aside small trees in his path. They had told the cat girl about Squiggles, but it is rather difficult to prepare someone for an encounter with a giant, winged, fire breathing lizard. To her credit, the girl doesn't scream, only backs into Alice before trying to turn and flee.

Alice holds her steady, "It's ok, it's ok. This is Squiggles."

The dragon looks to the boy, currently in Kaliska's arms, first, giving the cat girl a moment to adjust.

He opens his maw as if to accept his treat but Kaliska turns away, saying, "No, Squiggles. No eatcies today. Even better. We have new friends!"

Squiggles looks over the Chitali's shoulder at the boy and snorts disapprovingly. The Leeseran pup doesn't care for it and begins to cry, prompting the Feladine to come to him. She freezes when Squiggle turns his attention to her. The dragon looks from the Feladine and then to Alice placing herself at the younger girl's back.

"They're not for eating. They're friends," says Alice, putting her hands on the cat girl's shoulders.

The dragon cocks his head to one side and then sniffs about the girl. Braver than Alice had been at her age, the Feladine lifts a hand to Squiggle's nose. He pulls back slightly but then lets her touch his muzzle while he sniffs curiously at her. Eventually, he decides she is ok and gives her ears an exploratory lick.

The children have a chance to get better acquainted with Squiggles as they wait for dark. The cat girl makes a game of patting the dragon and then hiding behind his legs as he cranes his neck around to see her. She hasn't spoken yet but laughs when spotted. She also coughs more, which worries Alice. She shares this cough with the Leeseran boy, though Kaliska believes she can do something about it back at their camp.

Once darkness comes and it's safe to fly, Alice, Kaliska, and their two new companions board Squiggles. The slight added weight does little to hinder the dragon as they put feet and thighs through loops made of woven grass rope, while taking hold of reigns tied around the great reptile's neck and forelimbs. Alice sits in the lead with the Feladine directly behind her and Kaliska, holding the tiny squirrel boy, in the rear. They sit cramped tightly together just over Squiggles' shoulders and the cat girl must hold onto Alice's waist.

Situated, Alice gives the dragon a pat along his

neck, "Alright, let's go."

Squiggles rumbles and starts to flap his powerful wings. After a bit of warming up, he begins to run out into a clearing among the trees, flapping harder and harder. The cat girl's grip becomes steadily tighter around Alice's waist as the dragon picks up speed, the ride very bumpy. When he's ready, Squiggles suddenly leaps into the air. The move is expected by Alice but she still jumps in surprise when the Feladine's claws suddenly poke her stomach right through her clothes, the younger girl holding as tightly as she can. Alice lowers her elbows to rub along the girl's forearms, grinning back at her as the dragon ascends.

When Squiggles reaches his cruising altitude, the ride smooths considerably. Her claws retracted, the cat girl manages to relax enough to rest her head against Alice's back, bringing a warm smile to the Tokala. After a long ride, all are tired and Alice is grateful when she spots a fire, bright among the tall, dark trees. As they decend for a landing, two orange dots break away from the main fire and swing wildly in the darkness, Danahlia guiding them in.

The Liguna rushes over to greet her friends as

they touch down, "Hey! How'd it-?"

Twinkaleni calls forth a magical light over an upraised palm appearing beside the much taller girl, "Did you happen to acquire any pa-?"

Both are given pause by the extra passengers as Alice and Kaliska untangle themselves from straps and hand holds.

"Guys, look it!" Kaliska calls excitedly, presenting the cloth wrapped Leeseran.

Twinkaleni raises her magic ball of orange light higher to better illuminate them. "Is that, is that a child?" she asks, her large, round ears perking up.

"Yeah! Isn't he cute?" coos Kaliska to the small bundle. "He's sick, but we're gonna make him all better," the Chitali explains.

Danahlia moves to Squiggle's head, guiding him to lay down so the riders can dismount easier, while looking curiously at the cat girl, "Who's that?"

Alice slides down the dragon's side and then turns to help the Feladine. The girl's black fur makes her nearly indistinguishable from the dark save for her warily watching, green eyes sparkling in the mage's light. She lets herself be pulled to the ground but then shys behind Alice at the Liguna's approach.

"Some kids from town. They could use our help," says Alice wearily, reaching back to place a stroking hand over the cat girl's head. She flinches at the touch but stays focused on the Liguna leaning over before her.

"Huh, well hey there, Fuzzball," greets Danahlia. The Feladine tucks further behind Alice and the lizard girl takes a step back, "Can handle a few thousand pounds o' dragon but not me huh?" She then poses provocatively while running a hand down her body and over her curled tail, "I get it, too much beauty all at once. It's overwhelming."

The Feladine is made curious by this and tentatively steps out from behind Alice. Danahlia pauses, looking away but watching from the corner of her eye as the black furred girl lifts a hand to touch Danahlia's lengthy furless tail, completely regenerated after much of it was hacked off by bandits during the previous winter. She looks back and forth between Danahlia and the appendage as if to make sure the lizard girl doesn't take offense while she examines it closer.

"Like that huh?" asks Danahlia, giving her tail a little wiggle.

The girl says nothing but seems fascinated by the Liguna, likely the first Cold Blood she had ever seen. Squiggles rumbles his hunger and the tiny Leeseran coughs, so the girls make their way to the Hollow. During a meal, Kaliska fashions masks from strips of cloth. They have pockets filled with some concoction of dried, strong smelling herbs that the children are meant to breathe through. With their masks on, the Feladine wraps herself around the Squirrel pup and settles in atop the fur hides she had been given for bedding. Exhausted from their journey, the others soon follow suit.

Danahlia nuzzles Alice's ear playfully, "So, kids huh? You ready to be a parent?"

Alice's eyes widen, "I, I don't know. But what else could we do? We couldn't just leave 'em, sick and hungry. We'll have to feed them and cloth them and keep them safe. Teach them things. How to live out here and, ticks, how are we gonna do all that?

What if a bear or one of them falls and-"

Danahlia gives Alice a little kiss on the lips, stopping her fretting. "It's gonna be interesting," the Liguna agrees.

Chapter 4

Light

Over the next little while, Kaliska's herbal masks steadily decrease the young pair's cough until it's completely gone. The tiny Leeseran is still very weak from extended malnutrition and is often carried around by the girls when they go out foraging. With Kaliska's care, the squirrel boy gradually recovers, his bone thin body slowly building with much needed fat and muscle. Eventually he is able to crawl about some but still prefers to be held. He is very small, even for his age, but looks to be improving at least. The Feladine is nervous at first but very curious about her new home. She maintains her disinterest in words but makes sounds, gestures, and faces to indicate her interest or disapproval of things she sees, smells, touches, and tastes.

They come to call the cat girl, Jetta after her jet black fur. She still hasn't spoken but responds to the name when called. Jetta shares a love of fish that may rival Alice's own and is always eager to come on fishing trips with the other girls. Alice enjoys using her bow with a bit of rope tied to an arrow to fish while Danahlia prefers diving directly into the water to use her spear. They must use these mundane methods as Twinkaleni rarely breaks away from her study of the caves. Alice has more success in passing on her teachings to the young Feladine as Jetta doesn't like getting wet. After a time, Jetta is proudly able to catch, clean, and cook, her own supper.

The name "Narco" is given to the Leeseran after one of the herbs used to treat him. Gradually, he becomes a very energetic little boy. Kaliska has him under constant supervision as he tends to get himself into trouble if no one is looking. This is only compounded by his ceaseless curiosity about the world around him and his habit of trying to climb everything he can. In a forest with exceptionally high trees, this often leaves the tiny squirrel child in need of rescue once he realizes how high he's gotten. Despite this, he continues to do so and will sometimes use his ability to snack on fruits and nuts from branches that would otherwise break under the weight of anyone else.

Alice, Danahlia, and Kaliska do their best to teach the children things that will help them survive. Basics like keeping clean and fed are essentials. Alice and Danahlia also show the kids techniques for starting fires, moving silently through the woods, and tracking animals. They try to teach hunting as well but neither are enthusiastic about it, especially since Narco prefers Kaliska's vegetarian life style. The Chitali has a great deal of knowledge to offer on the subject of edible and medicinal plants, but is easily distracted by games she and the children play. Twinkaleni makes only infrequent and brief appearances before returning to her studies. Neither of the children are magically gifted and so she feels her efforts are better spent learning herself. She does however like to emerge when she's made a particularly interesting discovery.

On one such occasion, Alice and Jetta are returning from a nearby stream after catching some fish for supper. Jetta is especially proud this evening since she caught the biggest fish and was promised it all to herself. They see Kaliska and Narco, already by the fire roasting nuts while tossing already cooked ones into each others' mouths. They're not yet in hailing range when Danahlia runs in from the direction of the caves, moving and gesturing with great excitement. Kaliska stands with what looks like alarm and Alice's gut tightens a bit in worry.

Danahlia spots Alice with the Feladine and gestures for them to hurry, shouting, "Guys! Come on!"

Before Alice can shout back, Danahlia turns and dashes back the way she'd come with Kaliska, holding Narco, in pursuit. Visions of cave-ins trapping Twinkaleni or Squiggles flash through Alice's thoughts and she drops her catch to run after the Liguna, Jetta following.

Alice calls after the others, "Hey! Wait!"

But only gets Danahlia to shout back, "Hurry up!"

The caves are not far from their camp but running at full speed, Alice is still out of breath when she arrives to find Twinkaleni and Squiggles are just fine, the dragon even napping. Danahlia is pestering Twinkaleni while the diminutive mouse girl drinks from a water skin, insisting that the mage show them something. Jetta has held onto her fish and now shows it to Narco while Alice notices the stone heart in a clearing surrounded by other small stones loosely stacked into a pile. She asks Kaliska what's going on but the Chitali only shrugs.

After her drink, Twinkaleni grins, "Oh, very well."

As the Murin makes her way to the pile of stones, Danahlia turns to the others, "Check this out, check this out."

Before the pile, Twinkaleni flicks her wrists so that her too long shirt sleeves fall away from tiny, pink hands.

Still confused, Alice asks, "Is it magic?" but only gets shushed by Danahlia.

After a few moments of focus, her open hands directed to the pile with the stone heart, Twinkaleni sternly says, "Gaiadem."

With her word, the Murin mage slowly faces her hands toward each other as if trying to squish an invisible ball between them. While she does, the stone heart's misty, green glow brightens considerably, reaching out with wispy, transparent, green tendrils that wrap around the other rocks around it. Each rock so touched glows green as well and begins to roll toward the stone heart. The stones roll over each other and up, covering the stone heart while simultaneously lifting it a few inches from the ground. As the stone heart is encased, the glow dims and the roughly spherically shaped gathering of rocks sprouts two stubby legs formed from more rocks. More still gather to form two short arms, then even a few rocks gather on top to form a head. By the end of the rocks' movements, Twinkaleni has the general shape of a short, plump figure standing perhaps a foot tall in front of her.

"Is that, an elemental?" asks Alice, then to the children who approach it to she says, "No, Jetta, Narco, don't."

The cat girl gives pause but Narco is too curious and needs Kaliska to pick him up as Twinkaleni assures, "It's quite alright. It is completely under my control. This is a golem. Or at least it will be once I've refined my technique."

Alice looks to the Murin, "A golem?"

Before Twinkaleni can respond, Danahlia calls excitedly, "Do it, make it do it."

The mage grins and with added focus, she moves her splayed fingers toward the foot tall rock man like a puppeteer. And the golem moves. At first it takes a few stiff, awkward steps forward, nearly tumbling, but then rights itself and walks around in a tight circle. Twinkaleni has the stone golem move about some more as she explains that golems are magical constructs, creatures born of will, magic, and, in this case, earth. She says they differ from elementals in that an elemental is naturally created from ambient magic while golems are created through the skill of a magic wielder.

Twinkaleni has her golem march to where Kaliska holds Narco and the boy squirms until let down to investigate. Alice, Kaliska, and Jetta, join him, looking closely at the rock being.

Alice tosses a pebble and watches it bounces off the golem to no reaction, she then asks, "Is it alive?"

"Oh no, all that animates it is my will, channeled through the stone heart. It can perform no action not commanded by me. Observe," says Twinkaleni as Jetta swiftly bats at the golem with a paw before retreating. The Murin mage then lets her hands go limp and the golem crumbles back into a pile of stones and rocks, revealing the glowing stone heart in it's center.

"Mini-Mage can make elementals now," Danahlia says cheerily.

"Golem," corrects Twinkaleni, "Though I must admit, the foundation for such magic was already present in the stone heart, I merely manipulated it to my designs. Gaiadem." With the word, the Murin reaches out to the rubble and reconstructs her golem.

Alice recovers the fish she dropped and the older girls prepare supper. The children play with the golem, Twinkaleni having it chase them around, making it appear stunned when one of them tosses a pebble at it. The mouse mage goes on in length about the technique and experiments leading up to her new ability. It all sounds very impressive and complex to Alice, and the Murin is saying she still has a great deal to learn when Squiggles rouses from his nap. Perhaps pulled from slumber by the scent of cooking fish or the laughter of the children, the dragon makes a happy drumming noise in his throat when he sees the girls. As he rises, he spots the golem and immediately zeroes in on it.

Twinkaleni squeaks in alarm and has the round, stone man flee toward her as she in turn runs toward it. Squiggles closing, the mage drops her animating spell, letting the golem crumble once more, before reaching to it with one hand, calling, "Telefuss!" The stone heart flies free from the rubble just as Squiggles snaps at it, missing by a hair. Twinkaleni catches the glowing stone, tumbling to the ground while curling into a ball around it. Squiggles lets out a frustrated whine and nudges the mouse girl with his muzzle as she shouts for him to go away, slapping at his nose with one tiny hand.

Alice calls to the dragon, waving the fish she'd been cleaning. He eventually gives up on the Murin and lets himself be lured by the offering. As Danahlia helps up the mage, Alice tells Squiggles to sit. He does so, and then she calls, "Infermious!" Squiggles dutifully puffs a bit of fire over the Tokala's head and she rewards him with the fish and affectionate strokes along his neck. The children begin to climb over Squiggles, as they generally did whenever in his presence, while the dragon tries to get more fish out of the fox girl.

"Why's he want that so bad?" Danahlia asks, reaching for the stone heart.

Twinkaleni pulls it away, saying, "I do not care to know," before scampering off to secret her treasure away.

When the summer begins to cool, giving way to fall, the Cloudstalkers return. Hawk-like in appearance, the impressively winged Wakuwai tribes people make their annual migration back to the mountains from their summer camp near the sea, intent on hunting the large herds of ferals that pass through the Northern Plains each year in preparation for winter. Their arrival is marked with celebration and a feast thrown for them by the girls. They give generously from their stores of dried meats, something the Cloudstalkers, after a flight of many days, are grateful for. The feasting allows them to reunite with old friends like Lolani, a prominent member of the tribe who had led the rescue of the girls after some dreadful mountain bandits had kidnapped them, as well as introduce the new members of their little family, Jetta and Narco. The children are frightened of the bird people at first. With their powerful hooked beaks and large talons, the Ornivian tribe is one of hunters and warriors, but they are also a very welcoming people to those who treat them with respect and the children are soon playing with the younger members.

Almost immediately after arriving, the Cloudstalkers send out hunting parties to their traditional stations along the migrating herds' path, a distance south and south west. Despite the Gadara Mountains' abundant game, the bird people have difficulty hunting there. They prefer the open air to the massive, lush Zalonya trees they have made their homes in. This leaves mostly the elders and youngsters to clean out and settle into their winter homes. Alice and Danahlia decide not to hunt with Weiya, a young hunter in training, and Lolani this time, but instead occasionally visit them atop Squiggles to help haul their kills back to their main camp, saving the tribe a great deal of labor. Like their trade runs, this is only done at night.

Eventually, the changes to their sacred caves are discovered and the girls tell them that the mountain god's child that had inhabited them had sprung up from the cave and disappeared to the north, perhaps to be with it's parent, who the girls describe as the titan they had seen. Most of the tribe is skeptical of this but feel that if the mountain god's children have left the cave, then there is no harm in the girl's exploration of it, especially if Squiggles likes it. The Wakuwai themselves do not enter the caves, or any others. In fact, they rarely stay on the ground for long, favoring the freedom of the sky and the safety of their great trees.

Alice and Danahlia continue to hunt and gather during the fall in the hopes of storing enough for winter. Kaliska watches over the children while Twinkaleni continues her research and exploration of the caves. With the Murin's growing mastery over the stone heart, Pebbles, what the others call her golem, can be made steadily larger. The golem not only swells in size, but also changes shape, becoming more specialized at digging through the earth by forming large shovel like hands when rubble must be removed or sledgehammer like fists for breaking up rock. Over time, Twinkaleni relies less on Squiggles and more on her golem to excavate the elaborate mountain caves, going so far as to get the others to lure Squiggles away so he doesn't pester Pebbles. This gives the other girls the opportunity to fly Squiggles around the mountain, sometimes hunting, sometimes mapping out the region, and sometimes just for the sheer thrill of it.

During their second winter, Twinkaleni makes a new discovery.

"I believe I now know from where the steam in the caves emanates," she says from behind a cooked fish.

"Yeah? Where's that?" asks Danahlia, smacking on her own supper.

"Well," replies the Murin before going in detail about a tunnel, that had previously been unexplored, leading to another massive chamber. From what she says, it was filled with warm water, among other things.

"Other things?" Alice wonders, pushing Squiggle's muzzle away as he begs Jetta, sitting beside her, for her fish.

"More bugs?" Kaliska asks distastefully as she tosses berries into Narco's mouth, the boy atop the dragon's head using his horns as hand holds. Most of the berries miss, leaving little wet purple patches all over Squiggle's face, though his attention is fully on Jetta's dinner.

"Possibly," replies Twinkaleni, returning to nibble on her fish.

Danahlia grins, "Huh, so you ran before you could find out?"

Twinkaleni narrows her amber eyes at the Liguna, "I took a precautionary withdraw from a possibly dangerous situation."

"That was smart, Twinkaleni," says Alice looking sharply at Danahlia, "What *did* you see?"

"Little," replies the Murin, "The cavern was simply too great and I can only stretch a torch's light so far. But there was significant moisture in the air and the echo of splashing, suggesting water and the disturbance of it."

"Splashing, like a waterfall?" asks Kaliska.

Twinkaleni shakes her head, "No, too inconsistent. I believe there are life forms, possibly even another elemental. Which is why I must ask for your assistance."

The small mage explains her plan and the next

morning, Alice, Danahlia, and Squiggles accompany her down into the caves. Twinkaleni mostly wanted the others to help carry wood and such down into the steamy cavern. Too deep in the mountain to draw from sunlight, the Murin must borrow from fire to power her light magic. Having a dragon along couldn't hurt either. The tunnel isn't large and Squiggles must crawl on his belly for much of it, though he doesn't seem to mind, he's eager even, taking the lead and needing to be called by the girls to slow down.

Here we all go, goin' down a cave,

Couldn't go alone 'cause Twinkie's not brave.

We're goin' down to who knows where,

Probably should 'a brought fresh underwear.

Left our home, a nice little hut,

To follow behind this dragon's butt.

Goin' first might have been more smart,

'Cause ya' never know when a dragon might fart.

Alice giggles at Danahlia's silly song and they're shushed by Twinkaleni. "We're nearly there," she says after examining a mark she'd left on the wall with charcoal, "Keep alert."

They quite, all three carrying torches along with wood in their packs. Even Squiggles has some lumber wrapped in a hide dragging behind him from ropes tied around his hind legs. After another minute they enter a large chamber. Squiggles stretches out his wings, looking around in the pitch blackness excitedly. The dragon has exceptional night vision and immediately begins to wander off but is called back by the girls. He grumbles impatiently as the ropes are removed from him and then races off, disappearing into the darkness. The girls call to him but only hear his steps for a time, before they too disappear.

"Ticks, now what?" asks Danahlia, holding her torch to the darkness.

The ever present steam is even thicker here, this coupled with the dark greatly limits how far they can see. The air is wetter and warmer as well.

"I'm sure he'll be fine," says Alice, looking around.

"I'm not worried about *him*. I'm worried about *us*. I can't see a thing," admits Danahlia.

"We have a mission," reminds Twinkaleni, setting down her pack full of sticks, "Let us get a fire going."

They set up three fires in a crescent from where they entered the chamber. Twinkaleni stands between them and sends out bright balls of orange light to illuminate the chamber some. She sends them one at a time, borrowing from each fire in turn. When she does, the light from the fire dims considerably though the heat remains, making them look almost like the ghosts of fires. The mage sends her magical lights all around, including up, to get a scope of the chamber they've entered.

Pale skittering forms hurry away from the light, giving the girls glimpses as to what dwells in this murky domain. Many look to be insects with unsettlingly long limbs and searching antennae, while others might be lizards. There is splashing coming from somewhere, echoing around the chamber. As Twinkaleni had said, it's inconsistent, making Alice think something alive is causing it. Alice and Danahlia remain by the Murin's side, weapons drawn and torches held high as the immediate area is revealed to them.

Twinkaleni suddenly squeaks in panic, jumping surprisingly high into the air before dashing behind Danahlia's legs.

"What?! What?!" the larger girls demand, holding their weapons before them.

The mouse girl shudders, pointing into the shadow between two of their fires, "Something touched me!"

Alice sees a darker patch of shadow where the Murin indicates and lowers her torch. In the uneven light, they can see the tapered end of a long, slender stick leading out into the darkness beyond the light. It moves, waving back and forth while tapping at the stone like the cane of a blind man. Alice hurls her torch at where she thinks the other end of the stick might be, taking a two handed grip on her sword. The torch bounces off something hard and falls, the dim flame revealing the silhouette of several segmented legs, each as thick as the fox girl's wrists and not very far away. The legs rap on the stone floor, carrying something large off to the side, just out of the fire light. Danahlia tosses her own torch, leading it. Thick crab like pincers are revealed as her torch lands before it, the thing backing off, several sets of long insectoid antennae waving away from the flame.

"Oh, that's a big 'un," comments Danahlia, raising her spear in both hands. The girls gather closer together behind their fires, backs to the exit.

"What is that thing?" Alice asks shakily.

"I don't know, but it doesn't like fire, here," says Danahlia, taking a burning bit of wood from a fire and tossing it at the deeply shadowed monster.

Alice joins her and the monster skitters about, jerking away from the burning sticks though it doesn't give much ground. Twinkaleni forms a magic light and sends it to the creature. They all watch as the creature remains still, seemingly mesmerized by the orange ball. Twinkaleni has it float closer, revealing some hideously large, almost luminously pale crustacean.

As the magical orb hovers nearer, the girls can see it has many sets of legs of varying sizes, smaller ones tucked close while larger one are spread around it, all ending in points. Twinkaleni's light floats higher, revealing it also has several sets of claws. It's primary pair are unnaturally thick, nubbed and held open, silently following the light's progress. Smaller sets surround what Alice thinks might be it's mouth, dozens of them shifting around eagerly, some tentatively reaching toward the light. The light flies higher among a bristle of antennae, these too varying in size from very large to perhaps pinky thick. Just above these sprouts what Alice thinks is a battery of strange mushroom like eye stalks.

Before they can get a decent look, the perhaps seven foot tall monster swiftly snaps it's powerful pincers over Twinkaleni's light, snuffing it out and coating itself once more in impenetrable shadow. The girls jump at the sudden move and Twinkaleni shouts, "Feasta!" The flames from their fires dim to near nothing as a beam of heat and light flies into the darkness, hitting nothing while plunging the girls into near complete black.

"Ticks, Twinkie! You almost took out our light,"

Danahlia whispers hoarsely, keeping her spear pointed in the direction of the clicks coming from the monster's foot steps. The sticks and torches the girls threw are out but the three fires slowly flicker back to life, though greatly weakened from the mage's spell. "Use that brain poppin' one," the Liguna suggests.

Twinkaleni shakes her head, "I must see my target and it *must* remain still. Perhaps if you could hold it in the light."

Danahlia nods, "Yeah, I'll just ask *real* nice."

Twinkaleni pulls on the hem of Danahlia's shirt, her voice shaking, "We should retreat for now. We can return with more wood."

"What about Squigs?" asks Alice, not entirely rejecting the idea.

"He's a big boy, he can handle himself," says Danahlia backing away slowly toward the exit.

Alice back peddles with her friends, sword point waving to the darkness, "We can't just leave 'im."

"Oh, of course," says Twinkaleni, pulling out the stone heart from somewhere.

Danahlia glances to the glowing green rock, "Think Pebbles can take that thing?"

"I do not know, but the golem may slow it down. Keep it back for a moment," Twinkaleni orders. The small mage then tosses the stone ahead of her to the ground, pointing her tiny pink hands to it and calling, "Gaiadem!" The stone heart glows brighter, small rocks and stones beginning to roll toward it.

"Come on, come on come on come on," groans Danahlia, the rapid tapping of the monster getting closer.

"That is not helping," grumbles Twinkaleni, larger rocks pulling free from where they sit to join the slowly forming golem.

Alice sees movement in the darkness and squints, trying to see through the steamy black. She's about to call warning to her friends when a large claw clamps over their right most fire sending burning sticks and embers flying. They shout in surprise as a third of their struggling illumination disappears. Alice swings at the claw, but even the sharpened steel of her sword only glances off the thick carapace just before it retracts back into blackness. She hits the stone floor and the steel sings, vibrating painfully into her palms and causing weird echoes throughout the cavern.

Danahlia shouts, "SQUIGS! We could use some help over here!" as she and Alice try to follow the creature's rapping in the growing darkness.

Alice and Danahlia try to angle themselves to keep a fire between them and the creature while not leaving Twinkaleni open. The monster circles around again, using the gap left open by the fire it destroyed to get closer to the girls but Alice slashes at the center fire, sending a few burning sticks toward it. The creature's claws grab wildly at these as it retreats once more.

"Squigs!" Alice cries, backing behind their last fire, the creatures feet rapping just out of sight.

Danahlia gives Alice's shoulder a tug, "Come on, we need to get outta here."

"Only a moment, more," says Twinkaleni, her voice straining as she tries to rush the assembly of her golem, the legs and upper body already formed.

"No, we need to go *now*," commands Danahlia, pushing Alice toward the exit tunnel before reaching for the mage.

"Squiggles!" Alice calls again turning back to the massive chamber, her voice echoing.

Danahlia assures, "He'll be fine, let's goOHHH!"

Alice turns to see the Liguna flying backward into the darkness, a thick claw clamped onto her backpack.

"DANNY!" Alice and Twinkaleni cry together. Alice immediately grabs a burning stick from the fire and races after her, the Murin mage calling her name.

The sticks flickering flame is barely enough to illuminate the stick itself. Alice instead follows the clicking noises and frightened cries of Danahlia.

From the sounds, she should be right in front of her, but the darkness is so complete she can only wave her ember tipped stick frantically around, calling to her friend. Something knocks into Alice's legs, tripping her and she falls onto something hard, rough, and moving. The tiny light from her stick reveals she's fallen onto the monster's lobster like tail, it's scuttling legs shifting about around her. Alice manages to get a hand hold between two segments of it's carapace before she's rolled off. She then slides the tip of her sword in the thin slit at the base of it's tail and plunges the blade through as deeply as she can. The effect is immediate.

The creature jolts and whirls, furious clicking noises erupting from somewhere on it. It spins again and Alice nearly slips off, abandoning her hold on it's shell in favor of grasping her sword with both hands. She hears Danahlia cry out from somewhere nearby but the chamber is filled with so much rapping, clicking, and whirling, that it's all she can do to hold on. Warm fluids spill from the monster's wound, making Alice's grip less sure by the second. She tries grasping onto Jellybane's cross guard just as the monster bucks and twirls again sending her flying off. She smacks onto the cave's stone floor hard, rolling before having a moment to realize what just happened. In the split second it takes her to figure out she's face down, she finds she can see somewhat but before she can even process the thought, something hits her sharply in the side and she shrieks, sure the monster has her.

Instead, Danahlia falls over her with a pained grunt.

Alice feels the Liguna wiggling over her, "Danny?"

"Alice? You scream like a girl. Come on!" Danahlia yanks the Tokala up, half dragging her toward where Twinkaleni is holding the last of the fire light over her in a ball. Alice can't get her balance in the darkness and ends up tripping over Danahlia's tail, taking them both to the ground once more.

"Ticks!" Danahlia grumbles, wiggling partially under Alice now. "Stop playin' aro-AHH!" Danahalia screams.

Alice immediately thinks she's hurt the Liguna and tries to roll off of her only to see the crustacean like monster looming over them, it's many smaller pincers clacking together. It wastes no time, one of it's primary claws coming for them. Alice immediately tucks into herself and closes her eyes, not wanting to see the monster tear her apart.

She hears a hard crunch and thinks it's gone for Danahlia first. She screams, "Danny!" her eyes flashing open as unknown bits fall over her.

The monster's claw is held just over her, a large rock in it's grasp. Alice follows the stone to a another and then to Pebbles standing over her, headless and with only one arm but stalwart in its defense of the girls.

She hears Twinkaleni cry, "Run, you fools!"

Danahlia and Alice scramble to a crawl as the monster bears down on the golem's arm with such strength that the rock begins to crack. It's other powerful pincer takes Pebbles by the shoulder and crushes the smaller stone there. The golem's one arm crumbles to the ground as the monster snaps viciously at the rest of it, turning Pebbles into rubble that rains painfully down on the girl's backs as they frantically try to flee.

Danahlia cries out and Alice looks to find the lizard girl's leg pinned under a hunk of Pebble's tumbling body. Working together, they manage to kick it away only for more to fall over them as the monster relentlessly smashes it's way through the golem.

Twinkaleni cries, "Telefuss!" and some of the stones falling around them pause in midair before launching toward the monster. A few score hits before the creature displays an unsettling level of ingenuity by batting away any more flying rocks with its main claws before shielding its face while still snapping at the downed girls with it's smaller pincers. Alice and Danahlia cover their faces and kick at the ground, trying desperately to gain some distance while protecting themselves from falling debris.

Twinkaleni's voice comes from closer now when she shouts, "Siphvitae!"

Alice peeks through her fingers expectantly, but the monster only slows for a moment, snapping claws at the air before and around it as if attacking a swarm of gnats.

"I can't, hold it!" cries Twinkaleni as the monster seems to shake off her spell to resume it's pursuit of the girls.

Danahlia whips her long tail before them in a final defense as the monster's powerful pincers reach down for them, both girls screaming. Then the monster is gone. The girls look into the darkness, expecting at any moment for it to return and finish them off.

"What are you waiting for?! Move!" squeaks Twinkaleni, over the strange echoes bouncing all over.

Battered and bruised but able to rise, Alice and Danahlia run to the Murin and her light, the only source in the cavern.

As Danahlia runs past her, she pats the much smaller girl on the head, "Not bad, Twinkie. Maybe open with that, next time,"

Regrouping at the exit tunnel, Twinkaleni holds the light a little higher, "I could do little. The creature was quite resistant to my magic."

Panting, Alice asks, "So wha, what happened, to it?"

Danahlia waves them toward the exit, "Who cares, let's get the-" something heavy crashes to the ground beside them causing them all to jump. Twinkaleni's light goes out and returns to the last of their fires. In the flickering light, they see the thing is one of the monster's main claws.

Twinkaleni shakily answers Alice, "I believe, something larger, may have taken the creature."

"That's why, we gotta go," says Danahlia, grabbing a stick from the fire, reaching for Alice's arm.

Alice pulls away, "I can't, leave Jellybane."

Twinkaleni gathers the fire light once more into a ball and sends it slowly before them into the misty darkness where what now sounds like crunching and spattering is coming from.

"No, Twinkie, stop it! We gotta get outta here while we can! Let the thing that ate the other thing eat in peace!" orders Danahlia, preparing to pick the

Murin up in one hand. Then they hear a familiar grumble.

Twinkaleni speeds up her light ball until it falls on Squiggles, the monstrous crustacean, or what's left of it, in his mouth. He shakes it violently like a dog with a favorite toy, sending wet bits and chitin flying all over.

"Squiggles!" the girls call together racing toward the dragon.

Squiggles shows them some small interest before returning to his ravaging of the creature. He continues to shake it and claw at it until he bites it in half. He then stands over the monster, flapping his wings at it as if to show the girls what he has done, clearly very proud of himself.

"Better late then never, I guess," Danahlia mumbles, stopping before setting foot in the bits and pieces that used to be the imposing crustacean.

Alice steps before the dragon towering over her, fists in her hips, "We might have gotten killed! Where where you?! We needed you!"

Not understanding her words but seeing she's upset, Squiggles lowers his head and nuzzles the Tokala. Alice pushes him away, not in the mood, especially with his muzzle wet and sticky. Not only that, but she notices he's dripping with water for some reason, or what she hopes is water. He's also much warmer than the winter season should allow. Before she can say anything, Twinkaleni calls, "Telefuss!"

The green glowing stone heart pulls free from the pile left by Pebbles and flies toward the mage. With the speed of a cat, Squiggles bats the stone from the air with a fore paw and immediately dives his head after it, maw open.

Twinkaleni shouts, "No!" and pushes the tumbling stone in the opposite direction of Squiggles' lunge.

She then has it float over his head and back around to her as Squiggles searches frantically for it, squishing parts of the vanquished claw monster. Just as the stone reaches the Murin's outstretched hands, Squiggles clamps a few of his front teeth on it.

The dragon tugs, pulling the Murin several feet, causing her to loose control of her light spell before she plants herself to call "Telefuss!" once more. This jerks Squiggles' head forward with the magic stone but he refuses to release it, grumbling. Twinkaleni turns her head away from what Alice knows is truly foul breath and the two fight over the stone. Though fight seems an absurd word seeing as Twinkaleni is so small by comparison, all Squiggles does is hold still.

Alice begins searching for her sword in the near complete darkness, a glimmer alerting her to it's possible location, as Danahlia says, "Twinkie, maybe you should just give it to 'im, he did just save us."

"No!" the mage shouts stubbornly, before making sounds of disgust. Alice looks to see Squiggles using his tongue to try to push the Murin's tiny fingers off the stone heart.

"You're gonna lose a hand if you keep messin' with 'im over it," Danahlia insists, rummaging around the remains as well.

"He can't have it!" Twinkaleni squeaks, pulling

with all her tiny frame can muster.

Danahlia manages to find her spear and uses the butt of it to knock the stone heart from Squiggles' mouth, toward the Murin. Twinkaleni loses it but immediately falls over the tumbling stone, curling around it protectively.

Squiggles groans in protest but Danahlia just says, "Gotta be quicker next time, buddy."

Once Twinkaleni tucks the stone away, it's glow showing through her clothes, Squiggles looses interest in it, instead focusing back on the monster. He snuffles around the remains before nosily crunching on some choice bits. Twinkaleni conjures another light and Alice recovers her sword, wiping the goo covering the blade off on her trousers. She's greatly relieved to find it undamaged.

After a few moments to asses their wounds and catch their breath, the girls head back out, leaving the dragon to finish his meal.

Chapter 5

News

The girls spend much of the winter in and around the steam caves. It's warmer there and many of the creatures that dwell within turn out to be edible. Some are even quite tasty. Twinkaleni was right when she thought there was water in the deeper caverns. They find a few isolated springs but also a single vast subterranean lake, the water of which remains steam warm even in the depths of winter. Here, under the protection of Squiggles and Pebbles, they are free to harvest the many things that call this place home.

Among the organisms living in the caverns, they find some that resemble smaller versions of the monstrous crustacean from before, as well as long legged crab like creatures, blind but swift newts with long whiskers, and there are even fish living in the perpetually heated waters. Squiggles especially likes to keep warm by submerging himself in the lake and can often be heard splashing about in the echoing darkness. Nothing can challenge him here and so he roams freely, snacking and wandering.

When he is away, Twinkaleni summons Pebbles. Once fully formed, the golem is more than a match for the strange monsters of the steam caves, capable of swinging boulder sized fists at anything that appears threatening. Fortunately, the first monster seems to have been the largest of them and Pebbles is only kept active as a precaution.

Twinkaleni insists there is great power here, somewhere in the darkness, though Alice and Danahlia, unable to sense it, come mostly to explore and find food. The Murin mage attributes the creatures' natural resistance to her magic to this mysterious power, after having little luck influencing the cave dwellers directly with her spells. Even so, indirect uses, such as Pebbles' rock shattering punches, are still effective. Twinkaleni is also able to draw some on the power she feels, making her earth based magic, and thus Pebbles, stronger. As her skill with manipulating the golem increases, the small mage begins to ride Pebbles. Crafting a harness of stone where it's head would be, the Murin can direct the golem's efforts from a fortified height. Eventually, she is even able to readily change the golem's shape at will, allowing her to explore even smaller tunnels from the safety of her stone guardian.

Kaliska looks after Narco and Jetta while the others are exploring, though as they mark certain tunnels and chambers as safe, the children are also allowed into the mountain labyrinth. Various edible mushrooms and other fungi, some bioluminescent, grow in the caves, giving the children something to gather though mostly they play near the surface. Narco doesn't like the dark and remains close to the main entrance's fire, exploring nooks and crannies with Jetta, who tends to stay with him.

The girls spends many seasons in the mountains, bidding their Cloudstalker friends farewell in the spring and then welcoming them back again in the fall. Their confidence in their ability to survive grows, and as it does, so too does their small family.

Very occasionally, while on a trade run, they will spot a new young boy or girl in need, who they will invite back with them to their mountain home. Not all take the offer but those that do are made welcome, fed, clothed, and kept as healthy and happy as the girls can manage. In another year, they add an Echanian and a Lagomorph, the horse boy in his early teens, while the rabbit boy is still only a child. They even find a Cold Blood like Danahlia, a Molocie girl, though more accurately, she found them.

During a hunt, Alice and Danahlia were stalking a gathering of rather plump, flightless birds near the southern edge of the mountain forest. Fleet of foot, the birds had to be snuck up on, else they would break from feeding in the open for the safety of the trees. As Alice was lining up a shot, the birds suddenly charged at them, squawking in alarm. Never knowing the birds to be confrontational, Alice had dropped her bow to draw her sword as Danahlia readied her spear, but upon seeing the two hunters, the birds panicked, fleeing in all directions for the trees and leaving the young Molocie sagging from exhaustion in their wake.

The moment she spotted Alice, she had tried to flee. But starving and weary, she didn't get far. Danahlia spoke to her in a language Alice didn't understand, calming the girl. She only vaguely looks like Danahlia, smaller, terribly thin, and with skin like desert sand. Her tail is shorter and more vertical than conical like Danahlia's, and her head is a little wider with a shorter muzzle. They found she had been in hiding with her father, as many Cold Bloods were after the outbreak of the Blood War. A mob of Warm Bloods had found them and her father had told her to run north while he distracted them. That was several days before being discovered by Alice and Danahlia.

The girl's name is Perthi and she speaks a little Arsalian. Alice and Danahlia fed her, but she refused to go back to camp with them, determined to remain near the edge of the forest to keep watch for her missing father. Danahlia remained with the girl as Alice traveled between them and the Hollow on Squiggles to keep them supplied and to share the news with the others. Danahlia and Perthi placed markers the Cold Bloods use as code to help their kind navigate the dangerous Warm Blood lands on large rocks, trees and any other landmarks that might attract Perthi's father's attention. They kept watch for a week before Danahlia could convince Perthi to come to the girls' main camp. They never did find her father.

Perthi is welcomed by the other children, most too young to have much interest in the prejudices against her kind. Despite this and the fierce looking backward facing spines she has along her jaw line and forehead, she is a very timid girl, preferring to silently follow Danahlia around wherever she goes. The girls do their best to teach Perthi and the other children how to survive in their new home. As they had learned from the Cloudstalkers, dangerous tasks, such as hunting, are left to the more experienced while the children are taught to forage.

Kaliska begins to say that her goddess, Althea, had set her on this path, to save the children of the war, and makes it her personal mission to do all she can, actively seeking out those orphans in need whenever they stop in a settlement to trade. This makes it all the easier for Twinkaleni to gain her approval in seeking to rescue the young mages being brainwashed into becoming obedient weapons by the Order of Thermathrogi.

The Murin had often mentioned returning to the Order to liberate her kind but always in a future tense, saying they weren't ready yet and that they needed more time to prepare. Because of this, Alice and the others had largely ignored it, figuring this was some plan she was concocting for sometime far into the future which could have no bearing on them now, especially with so much to do. But recently, the mouse girl has been talking as if the time was nearing. She often refers to Squiggles as being nearly large enough or her powers nearly strong enough. One evening at dinner, the mage announces that she wants to sneak into the Order of Thermathrogi's academy at Klepor.

After a few choking coughs, Danahlia bursts, "You wanna what? Where?"

Twinkaleni stands from the rock she sits on, though her height changes little, "I believe it is nearly time for an attempt on the Order. I wish to make contact with the mage's in training to gauge their receptivity to the idea of freeing themselves from it and joining us."

Alice frowns at the mage, "That sounds dangerous, and why Klepor? That's way down south."

Twinkaleni nods, "We will take measures to minimize the potential dangers, of course. Klepor houses the academy in which I was trained. I know it's halls and may even be remembered by some of the other mages. It is the ideal target to begin the liberation of the magic wielders held under the oppression of the Order."

Danahlia points a half eaten drumstick at the Murin, "Might be remembered by your old teachers too, and the guards or whatever."

"Possible," Twinkaleni acknowledges, "Which is why we will utilize stealth to gather intelligence first."

Before the Murin can continue, Kaliska breaks away from the children's singing of a song about bears and berries to sniff toward the girls. The Chitali sniffs at the air as if following a scent before saying, "Something just got serious over here."

"Twinkaleni wants to sneak into the Order soon," informs Alice.

"To rescue the magic kids? Oh, I'm in!" cheers Kaliska.

"You would serve better here," says Twinkaleni, "Caring for and preparing the children we already have. I believe Alice, Danny, Squiggles, and I will be adequate for this task."

"What are *we* supposed to do?" asks Alice.

Twinkaleni sits back down on her rock, "For now, I would like only for you to listen."

Twinkaleni outlines a plan involving Alice and herself venturing into Klepor, a sizable city in southern Arsalia. The girls had avoided larger settlements for the most part do to the dangers they posed, but now the Murin wanted to purposely enter one of the largest in the kingdom. They would ride Squiggles there, then Danahlia would keep the growing dragon hidden in a nearby forest, one the Murin had hidden in herself when she had first escaped the Order. Alice and Twinkaleni would make their way to the Order of Thermathrogi's academy building, remaining inconspicuous while checking for possible avenues of entry. Once found, they would attempt to enter under cloak of night and make contact with the mages kept imprisoned there.

Discussion continues over the course of many days as refinements to the plans are made and possible dangers are adapted to. Alice and Danahlia have difficulty becoming enthusiastic about the entire affair. It wasn't that they didn't feel for the children Twinkaleni insists are being enslaved by the Order. It was how dangerous going up against such an organizations would be. Twinkaleni had often described the Order of Thermathrogi as a place where minds were warped, lives were lost, and weapons were made. A place that had no misgivings about taking innocent children from their parents and making them feel so horrible about their gifts that the only way they could possibly have an existence of any worth was to become powerful mages that served only the will of Arsalia's monarchy. Allowed to live and learn the ways of magic solely so it can be used to destroy others and enforce rule.

The mages produced by the Order were an enormous asset to Arsalia's armies. As such, any attempt to disrupt production would be severely punished. The girls had already bore witness to the cruelty and abominable disregard for life the Order was capable of toward anyone who does not serve their interests. Because of this, Alice and Danahlia take care in trying to come up with reasons as to why antagonizing such people is too dangerous for them. Twinkaleni, however, remains convinced that they must act while they can, and soon.

The Murin insists that an attempt on the Order will only be successful while the Blood War strains their resources. While the war continues, most of the fighting men would have been incorporated into the army, which meant there would be fewer guards protecting the Order's academies. Not only this, but the pressure put on the Order to produce more skilled mages for the front lines would mean potential mages would be constantly brought in and more experienced ones sent out at a pace that would make it more difficult for the masters of the Order to keep track of all of their students. These, Twinkaleni believes, are key weaknesses that the girls *must* exploit.

Thoughts of so dangerous a task weigh heavily on Alice's mind, even as she stands in line for bread on another trade run. Bread was unnecessary, as the girls and their growing number of orphans, could live just fine off the bounty of the Gadara Mountains, but Alice had discovered that this particular baker made some of the finest bread she had ever had. Unfortunately, the locals also knew of it, which meant there was always a line. Still, the scent of the dried fish, garlic, and butter mixed into his loaves drew her in as readily as it had the very first time she caught hint of it on the air. It had become a habit to buy a few loaves whenever they visited the small town and had any money left over from more necessary trades. The children had even come to eagerly anticipate it.

Even the delightful scent of her favorite bread permeating the streets was doing little to alleviate Alice's concerns for the girl's upcoming quest to Klepor, which is why it startles her when she hears the rough bellow of a man calling, "Hey, girl!"

Alice jumps a little and looks around to find a Bovidan man seated but turned away from from a table set before a neighboring building along the street, looking right at her. He grins when she spots him. After an encounter with a deplorable group of mountain bandits, Alice had become especially wary of strange men and immediately looks away, unable to imagine the stranger having anything of worth to tell her.

"Hey, girl! Come 'ere a moment. Let me get a look at 'cha," the bull man tries again, his voice deep and resonating while jovial. Still, Alice decides to ignore him. Unfortunately, the line for her favored bread is long and slow, giving the man plenty of time to continue calling, "Oh, don't be like that. I'd come to ya but this stump o' mine makes walkin' a bit of a chore."

Alice gives the man another glance and sees he is missing much of his left leg, one of his long horns seems to have been broken off at some point as well. The bull man is large, even for his kind, and sits alone before what looks like a tavern, a pair of makeshift crutches propped in easy reach. Even so crippled, he is thickly muscled, tan and brown coated with a heavy looking bronze loop earring pulling down one teardrop shaped ear. He is simply clothed and smiles warmly at her attention.

Alice turns back to her line and the man calls again, "Come now, I just wanna see ya. Big T ain't no trouble, an' if I am, you can always walk away. Not like I can catch up. You remind me of someone I knew." Alice continues to ignore him, considering just leaving the line to go look for Kaliska. He continues, "The ears, the arms, the feet, and even the tail." Alice immediately tucks hers out of the man's view, but then he says the one thing, the one name that could make a breath catch in her throat, "You wouldn't happen to be a relation of ol' Robert Dippleblack, would ya?"

Robert Dippleblack was Alice's father. Years ago he was lost in the war that had also claimed her mother, leaving Alice alone in the world. It had been so long since she'd heard his name that she'd almost forgotten what it sounded like. She must have reacted visibly because the man's voice becomes excited, "Alice? Are you Alice Dippleblack?"

Thoughts, possibilities, questions, feelings, and more race through the young fox girl's mind, causing her to freeze. No one but her friends and the children knew her by name. Why would this man? Why would he know her father? Immediately thinking this is some sort of trap meant to lure her in, Alice considers leaving again, but her curiosity keeps her in place. Alice and her family had never lived this far north as far as she was aware. What could the Bovidan know of her and her father? Did it matter? He's gone and the words of some hobbled bull would not bring him back. Would it hurt to ask though?

Before Alice can decide on any action, she gets a little tap on the shoulder. She jumps, startling the impatient patron in line behind her before they gesture for her to move forward. Now before the baker, it takes her a moment to remember why she was in line at all. After a few dumbfounded, uh's, she eventually manages to purchase her bread and then walks off, not really sure what to do next, while keeping the man in the corner of her eye. After pacing in the street for a minute, she finally decides asking would be no great danger. The man could not give chase despite his size, and even if he had companions, they surely would do nothing in the open with so many witnesses about. Alice walks slowly toward the man, looking around to see if anyone is paying any mind, but the only one interested in her seems to be the man himself.

Keeping a cautious distance, Alice asks the grinning bull man, "What do you know about my-, Robert Dippleblack?"

The bull man's grin shows more teeth, "I happen to know plen'y, little lady."

Alice waits for him to elaborate but when he doesn't she asks, "Well?"

"Well, ol' Rob is a dear friends o' mine," the Bovidan says, raising his chin and scratching his neck, "and I only share stories about friends with other friends, see. Now, you wanted to be friends, well, then we'd have to introduce proper."

Alice glances around cautiously, "Oh-kay?"

The bull man grins wider, extending a large, beefy hand, "Well then, my names, Toreander Beuford Telenahee. Though most folk just call me, Big T."

Alice approaches the large man slowly, one hand reaching out of sight to the knife sheathed at her back while the other extends to the man's. She grips three powerful fingers and is given a little shake, as she says, "Nice to meet you, Mr. Telenahee. I'm-"

"Alice Dippleblack," Mr. Telenahee finishes for her, releasing her hand. Alice releases the handle of her knife. "Knew it the second I saw ya, I did. Got your daddy's colors. Ain't never seen a man so proud o' his little girl. He'd just go on and on about you all the time. Tell me though, the way Rob told it, y'all was livin' some place down south, Poki, Moki...,"

"Toki," Alice corrects, relaxing a bit when she sees no hint of malice in the man's eyes.

He points a thick finger at the young Tokala,

"That's the one. So what 'chu doin' way up heya?"

"Uh," Alice stalls, not wanting to reveal too much of herself to a stranger. She considers and then remembers her bread, "Me and my mom, moved up here. But not here here, a nearby village. Little place, to the... east. They don't have good bread there so, I'm on a bread run."

Mr. Telenahee nods, "Oh, I gotcha, I gotcha. How *is* your momma doin'? Must be hard without-"

"You said you knew my father?" Alice interrupts.

"Oh aye," Mr. Telenahee looks upward in fond remembrance, "Met him during my little stint in the war. Best swordsman I ever saw. Went into quite a few skirmishes wich' your old man. Boy, I can tell you some stories. Don't know how many times we fought 'gainst odds and came out on top. I recall one battle where-"

"Were you there when he...?" Alice's voice breaks and her vision begins to blur for some reason.

"When he got taken?" Mr. Telenahee asks somberly, "To mah ever lastin' shame, I was not." Alice's shoulders sag as he continues, "Took an arrow in the leg. Kept fightin' even with it, I ain't no quitter, see. 'Ventually though, the rot set in, then the butchers had to take it off. That was all the war Big T was meant for."

Alice feels her lower lip quiver and sets her jaw against it, "So... you didn't see him..."

"No, I didn't, but I guarantee he gave those Smoothies a merry chase, quick as your pop was," Mr. Telenahee says, brightening.

"Oh, who you buggin' nah?" another man's voice comes from behind the large Bovidan. Alice looks to find a lanky Rotan with an eye patch, holding two mugs and two bowls of something steaming, heading her way.

"'Eugene, you ain't never gonna believe who we got heya," Mr. Telenahee bellows.

"Looks like some kid you borin' witcher stories," grumbles the rat man, setting a bowl and mug before the Bovidan before taking a seat with his own meal.

"Quite 'cher yappin' an' take a good look see. Tell me she don't remind you o' someone," says Mr. Telenahee, gesturing to Alice before taking a drink from the mug before him.

Eugene looks at Alice with his one good eye. The eye widens for a second but then he dismisses her to lift his mug, "I 'on't see nothin'."

Mr. Telenahee gives his companion a slight shove, nearly making the Rotan spill on himself, "You a fool then. This is Rob Dippleblack's pup."

With his mug still before his lips, Eugene says disinterestedly, "Can't be. Rob hailed from down south. Boki, Koki-"

"Toki," Alice and Mr. Telenahee say together.

"Or some damn place," the Rotan continues, "No sense in 'er bein' all the way up heya."

"You git, are you blind?" Mr. Telenahee exclaims, then getting a sharp look from his one eyed companion, "Oh, right. Well it is. Alice

Dippleblack, this here is Eugene Striptail."

Eugene gives Alice a slight nod but seems far more interested in his meal, letting Mr. Telenahee go on, "Was just tellin' the lass what a hero her pop was. Best swordsman outta any o' us. We knew it, Smoothies knew it. Damn shame what happened to 'im. Damn shame. I am sorry, lass. If it weren't for this," he waves a hand at his stump of a leg, "I'da gone back myself, alone if I had to. I'da gone back."

Eugene nods along before adding, "We was supposed to go back. That was the plan. We were suppose to go back for 'im. But those tuckin' cowards up top, ain't even do no fightin'. Now why we need to listen to d'em anyhow? If they had any idea how to carry on a war it'd be over and done with by now."

Mr. Telenahee nods along this time and Alice asks, old grief fueling new anger, "You left him? Alone? Why?"

The men look to each other, shame in their expressions, and tell Alice the story of her father's last courageous act.

The war had been going favorably for Arsalia due to winter being particularly harsh on the Cold Bloods. Arsalia's armies took full advantage, swiftly taking a great deal of territory that had been harshly fought over for much of the past year. But with the seasons changing, the cold blooded Feorians were shaking off the effects of winter and had rallied, stopping the Arsalian advance into their country. Before the Warm Bloods could dig into the newly acquired lands, the Feorians began to ferociously push them back.

At an advantageous choke point along the southern front called the Nearthrough Falls, Robert Dippleblack, along with Telenahee, Striptail, and a small detachment of soldiers had just barely managed to hold off a Cold Blood advance force. Many of the Arsalians were wounded and scout reports said more Feorians were amassing for another attack, one more than capable of wiping out the remaining Warm Bloods. The officer in charge decided retreat would be the best course, to get the wounded to safety and return with more men. But with so few able bodied soldiers left they would have to leave many of the wounded behind, less they move too slowly and get overtaken by the approaching Cold Bloods.

To save his men, Robert Dippleblack made a choice. He would remain behind to hold off the Feorians for as long as he could, allowing his comrades to escape. Mr. Telenahee goes on in length of how skilled Alice's father was, how many Cold Bloods he'd felled, how they would have needed an army to take him, and how no one but he could have done what he did.

Eugene nods in agreement before adding into his bowl, "Saved us all he did. And what we do to thank 'im? We left 'im behind, that's what. Left 'im, like each and every one of us didn't owe 'im our lives two times over by then."

Alice fights hard to keep tears from showing, and is surprised at the harshness of her own voice when she asks, "Why?"

Mr. Telenahee looks down at his bowl on the table, "Wasn't nothin' we could do. By then my leg was gettin' too bad to walk on and Eugene just lost his eye and a few fingers."

Alice hadn't noticed before but sees the Rotan is missing his index and middle fingers on his right hand. Still she persists, "But what about the others? That officer, he said he was going to go back once he got more men, right? Why didn't he?"

Mr. Telenahee frowns deeply, unable to meet the young girl's gaze, "Way I hear it, the commanders felt we pushed too far too fast. We was spread too thin ya see, an' getting' hit all over. Decided to pull back and regroup before the lines broke."

"We was supposed to go back," grumbles Mr. Striptail disgustedly into his bowl, "He was expectin' us to. 'Stead we just up and left 'im."

"You let him die so you could save yourselves. You're cowards. You're cowards!" Alice shouts, unable to hold back her anger and tears anymore.

"Hey, easy now," says Mr. Telenahee, reaching for the distraught Tokala.

Alice steps out of reach to scream at the men, "YOU'RE COWARDS!"

Mr. Striptail doesn't argue, his head low, though Mr. Telenahee raises his voice, "Hey! We ain't let 'im die. We ain't," the harshness in his voice makes Alice jump and he softens it some, "Rob made a choice that made 'im a hero to us all. Ain't nothin' no one could'a done to stop 'im. That's the way your pop was. Always the first one up to do the missions ain't no one else got the gut to. Thinkin' if he do all he can, maybe the war be over just a lil' faster."

"He ain't did it for us though, not for the men, not for the army. Naw. He did it for you," Mr. Striptail nods at Alice, "Always talkin' 'bout getting' back to ya. Lookin' forward to teachin' ya this and that. Always goin' on about how we ain't here fightin' for the king, or the land, or the money, or any o' that mess they be tellin' us to be fightin' fo'. We here fightin' for you. Fightin' for our own families, our own pups, our own grand babies. All the way out here fightin', so that maybe, just maybe, they won't got to."

Alice listens to the man's wavering voice, watching the moist spots sprinkle the loaf of bread in her hands, the edges of it crushed under shaking fingers.

"'Sides, ain't nobody said he was dead," Mr.

Telenahee adds, his voice lifting.

"Now don't you go fillin' her head with that," Mr. Striptail warns.

"Ain't nobody saw it," Mr. Telenahee counters, "See, your pop was pretty well known by then. Ta us *and* the Smoothies. Now say what you want about Eggers, but one thing they ain't is dumb."

"Don't, T. Ain't no sense in it, given 'er this hope for nothin'," Mr. Striptail insists.

"If we ain't got hope, then what all we got?" Mr. Telenahee tosses back to his companion, and then to Alice says, "Like I said, your pop was the best sword we had, and the Smoothies knew it. Your pop knew it too. That's why it had to be him. See the Barebacks have a reputation for taken our best when they can. Like to take 'em prisoner so they can learn from 'em. Learn how we fight and get all the better themselves for it."

Alice looks up to the bull man, "He, might be alive? But the letter we got said he, died."

Mr. Telenahee lets out an exasperated sigh,

"S'what they tol' us. Probably so nobody try to go after 'im. Ol' Rob was a hero and well liked by us nobodies. But the higher ups didn't care for 'im much. Felt like he was takin' they glory and such, sayin' things they ain't like."

After a drink, Mr. Striptail adds, "Gold hides. All they money buys 'em shiny armor, but ain't nobody sellin' a cure for pride."

"So, you're sayin', my dad, might still be alive?" Alice asks, sniffling wetly.

Mr. Telenahee grins, "I bet my last leg he is. Somewhere in Feoria, given them Eggers a time while they try to get his secrets."

Mr. Striptail only sighs.

Mr. Telenahee goes on to tell Alice of his theory of what happened at the Nearthrough Falls, how Robert Dippleblack had bought his men time to escape while being chased all over by the Cold Bloods, possibly even hiding out there for a time, waiting for reinforcements that would never come. Eventually, maybe he was captured or even turned himself in, knowing it would be the smart thing to do. Mr. Telenahee assures Alice that they wouldn't have killed him if they could help it, he was too valuable to them alive.

After a few more stories about her father, Alice leaves the men and wanders to where she is suppose to meet Kaliska. With so much on her mind, she looses her way several times. She wonders if she should dare even think as Mr. Telenahee, spare the hope that her father might still be alive, somewhere. It had taken a great deal to accept his loss and Alice did not want to revisit those feelings. But now the possibility was there and she couldn't just forget it.

Chapter 6

The Order

For several days, Alice keeps what she heard from the men to herself, desperately wanting to believe in the possibility but afraid to allow the hope. Danahlia had noticed she'd been acting out of sorts and when they can get a free moment to themselves, the Liguna invites her to one of the cave's hot springs. It was one of the safer ones the girls had previously cleared of undesirables. Still they keep their weapons close and a fire burning nearby.

The springs are a wonderfully luxurious find in the mountains. Kept perpetually warm by yet unknown means, the waters have an incredibly relaxing and rejuvenating affect on the girls. Twinkaleni even says there is some magic in the water that aids in this. Kaliska feels it too and the children are often led down into the caverns for baths. For now though, Alice and Danahlia share this late night bathe alone.

The spring they choose is not large or deep,

the hot water seeping up through a crack between some stones. Twinkaleni has placed several stones she had enchanted in each of the springs the girls used, their faint green glows letting them see that the water is clear of threats. The pair bathe by fire light and then sit beside each other atop a submerged rock shelf to relax.

"You ready to tell me what's wrong yet?" Danahlia asks, using her tail to pull Alice a little closer. She had asked many times, but Alice had kept insisting that nothing was.

Finally Alice concedes, asking back, "Is it true that the Cold Bloods capture Warm Blood soldiers to take prisoner and learn from 'em?"

Danahlia cocks her head to one side, "What?"

"I heard they do. Do they?" Alice asks, looking into the Liguna's confused eyes.

"Uh, I don't know. Maybe. Why?"

"I met some men on the last trade run. They said they knew my dad, even fought with him. They told me what happened to 'im. They said that the

Cold Bloods might have taken my dad to try to learn how he fights. That he might still be alive."

"Whoa," Danahlia gasps.

"Is, is that something they do?" Alice asks more urgently, "Could he still be alive?"

Danahlia shakes her head, "I, I don't know. I was never in the army. I got stuck over here as soon as the war started remember?" Alice's body slumps and the Liguna takes the fox girl into her arms, "It could be true though."

Alice rests her head on Danahlia's ample chest, "What if it is? That would mean he's been a prisoner all this time. My mom..."

Danahlia holds Alice tighter, nuzzling her chin over the troubled fox girl's head, "If it is, maybe when the war's over, he'll come back."

"But what if it's not," Alice says glumly, "I don't wanna get my hopes up. I don't think I could take it if I went back to Toki to wait for him again and he never comes."

"Yeah, would be rough," Danahlia agrees.

"I just wish there was some way we could see. Maybe ride Squiggles to Feoria and ask around?"

"We could try that."

"But that's crazy, theirs no way they'd help a Warm Blood now."

"Yeah, they're not too happy with you furries at the moment."

"Plus, they might wanna take Squiggles."

"Probably."

Alice rubs her muzzle along Danahlia's neck, "I just don't know what to do. Why can't this war be over already?"

Danahlia kisses one of Alice's triangular ears, "I-" But she's cut off by Twinkaleni's voice coming from somewhere.

"Apologies for the intrusion," the Murin mage says as she rounds a corner with a magic light held over her.

Alice drifts away from Danahlia asking, "Twinkaleni? What're you doin' here? You should be in bed by now."

"I was just on my way back up when I heard your voices," the mage confesses.

"Dang it, Twinkie. You know what happens to little mages who don't get to bed on time?" Danahlia asks, irritated.

"What?" Twinkaleni huffs.

"They barge in on people's private time, that's what," Danahlia exclaims.

The small Murin crosses her arms over her chest, her light floating just over her head, "Again, I apologize, but I believe I may offer a solution."

Apparently having heard much of their conversation, Twinkaleni brings up her plans to free the mages from the Order of Thermathrogi once more.

"Geez, Twinkie, not that again," grumbles Danahlia as the girls dry themselves and redress.

"Listen. Taking the possibility of future battle mages from the Arsalian army will weaken it's resolve significantly. Success in liberating my fellow magic wielders may even force Arsalia to seek an end to the war. By now, both Cold and Warm Blood armies are no doubt exhausted but neither wishes to appear weak by offering terms. Our success may bring a swifter conclusion to the conflict by forcing Arsalia to do just that. This means prisoners will be exchanged and, Danny, you may even be able to return to your homeland at long last."

"An end to the war," Alice whispers.

"You're dreamin', Twinkie," assures Danahlia, "If we got caught, we're all dead. And since I'm a Cold Blood and you two would be traitors, they'd probably torture us long and hard first, just to make an example."

As the three make their way back to the surface, Twinkaleni continues trying to convince them of the merit of her plans. Danahlia remains unswayed but Alice is beginning to seriously reconsider. Twinkaleni persists in making her case for the group to commit, and with Kaliska's approval and Alice coming over to there side, it isn't long before all three are encouraging Danahlia to get on board with the idea. Danahlia's argument for the girl's safety slowly erodes under the assault and she finally gives up, agreeing only if the others take things slow and all precautions are taken.

Over the next weeks, the girls prepare for their dangerous mission. If things go well, they may be absent for a time, and so they gather enough food for themselves as well as Squiggles. They tell the children they will be leaving them under Kaliska's care and that the Chitali has the authority of Alice, Twinkaleni, and Danahlia. Some of the children, Perthi especially, want to go too, but the girls stress the danger of their mission, though withhold the details, saying only that it's success may mean more children will be joining them.

The day they intend to set out, Alice and Danahlia run off on one last "hunting trip." Upon arriving back at the Hollow in the evening, they are met by Twinkaleni, followed by a few of the children.

"Mmm, I see you've come back empty handed," greets the Murin mage.

Alice and Danahlia share a smile as Danahlia answers for them, "Yeah, critters were just too quick today."

"Indeed. I imagine it would have been rather difficult to bring anything down without these," the mouse girl directs them to their weapons, left in camp.

"Oh, uhhh..." Danahlia stalls.

"Um, we were just checkin' some traps today, didn't need 'em," says Alice.

Twinkaleni nods knowingly, "Right. In any case, I've taken the liberty of recharging the enchantment on your sword, Alice. I do not know how effective my efforts were but it may prove useful if our quest calls for it."

"Really?" Alice exclaims, jogging to Jellybane and pulling it from it's leather sheath. The broadsword looked as it always had, but upon taking it up, Alice feels the slightest sort of humming vibration from it. Alice's sword had originally been enchanted by pixies, giving it a magic that made the blade glow and when soiled, clean itself. After extensive use, the energy powering these effects had been drained.

Alice runs the tip of the blade in the dirt, then holds it up. The blade glows green and the earth staining it falls away, leaving it looking freshly polished. The children make exclamations of amazement, as they always did whenever Twinkaleni made any display of her power.

Alice joins them, "Wow, Twinkaleni, you did it! It's just like after the pixies enchanted it."

Twinkaleni grins as Danahlia wonders, "This mean you can enchant stuff now? How 'bout my spear? Having it light up would be wags for in the caves."

"Or the bow, could you make it shoot fire arrows or something?" Alice adds.

The mage raises her hands, shaking her head, "No, and no. I do not yet have such skill. I simply energized the enchantment already placed on

Jellybane. Speaking of which." Twinkaleni rummages around in a pocket to pull free a ring. "I've re-energized the ring of firebolts as well, though it is difficult to say how many charges it has." She holds the ring out to Danahlia.

Danahlia grins widely, reaching for it, "Wags! I've been missin' this thing."

Twinkaleni pulls it away from the Liguna, "This is meant to be a last resort. Using any magic recklessly is incredibly dangerous."

Danahlia swiftly snatches the ring from the Murin's hand, "Yeah, like you're one to talk, oh lady of the rock people."

After the evening meal, the departing trio give the children and Kaliska their farewells. Kaliska assures them that the children will be well looked after. The Chitali had truly taken to caring for the children and Alice knows they're in good hands. They don't plan to be gone a terribly long time, but saying good bye is still difficult. Once they're on their way, the girls ride Squiggles to the foot of the Gadara Mountains. There, they wait until full dark is upon them before the dragon takes flight from the forest, south to Klepor.

Since they only risk flying at night, the girls spend the trip hopping from one thick forest to another, remaining concealed among trees during the day. With her experience from trade runs, Alice can guide them for a time, but once they travel further south than she has gone, they must risk entering villages to get directions. Danahlia is left with Squiggles while Alice and Twinkaleni seek the villager's aid. Even flying swiftly by night, the journey takes several days, but eventually, the girls reach the vast city.

Alice had never seen a true city and is amazed to see how far the torches, candles, and lanterns of it's inhabitants stretch over the land.

As Squiggles hovers in the silhouette of a tall hill, Alice exclaims, "That's all one city? It's huge!" They have to talk loudly over the beat of the dragon's wings.

Twinkaleni replies, "Indeed. A benefit of it's size is that we will draw little notice. Let us find a spot to land."

"Aye, aye!" calls Danahlia from upfront, guiding Squiggles lower.

The girls are glad to set down in a forest some distance from the extensive reach of Klepor. Summer had already peaked and strong night winds had been making swift flying a chilly affair. So many nights of solid flight have also exhausted Squiggles and he is highly praised for his efforts. As morning sets upon them, the girls find a small stream for the dragon to take water and have a snack. Immediately after, Squiggles curls up in a clearing to nap. Twinkaleni and Alice leave Squiggles in Danahlia's hands to make their way through the forest and on to the vast city.

For safety, Squiggles and Danahlia are left a full day's walk from Klepor's furthest suburbs. Farm land surrounds the city and the girls steadily venture through it. Fields are slowly replaced by more and more houses until the later dominate. Alice and Twinkaleni make their way along the bustling streets wearing hooded cloaks of dark brown to keep from attracting attention as well as concealing their various provisions.

Klepor is a maze of streets, buildings, and

people, making it difficult for the girls to find their way. As they wander on, Alice can see that the city hasn't fared much better and in fact seems worse off then many other settlements. Beggars are numerous and patients for anyone interrupting anyone else's day with questions is thin. Still, Twinkaleni recalls little of her flight from the city and the girls must ask frequently of the locals for directions. This amounts to the pair following vague finger points and sometimes less savory gestures through the city.

It seems Klepor was built on a few wide hills, the poorer districts and slums surrounding more prosperous areas sitting at higher elevations. Entering these, they find the number of beggars decreasing but the girls also begin to notice city watch patrols. They do their best to avoid suspicion, but eventually one shouts, "Ey!"

The girls freeze as a Lutarin man with a club at his side and a purple embroidered uniform approaches them.

"No beggin' 'ere girls. Try the temples on Almsday," he says.

"We live here, sir, we're just trying to get home," replies Alice.

"Do ya now?" the otter man asks, and with startling agility, grabs both Alice and Twinkaleni by an arm each, "Tell me then, where's home sweet home for ya? Such a gentleman am I that I'll give ya a personal escort. Never know what kind'a unsavory sorts might be lurkin' about." Instinctively the girls tug away but the man has an iron grip.

"You are gracious to offer, but I feel we've already taken up too much of your time. Our houses are not far at all," explains Twinkaleni.

"That bein' the case, it won't be takin' but a minute er two then," says the Lutarin, pulling the girls along side him.

Alice directs the man for a block before pointing down an intersection, "She lives over there. My house is that way." Alice points down another street.

"Right then, you first," the man says, pulling them along the way Alice said her house was.

About half way down the street Alice hears Twinkaleni whisper under her breath, "Telefuss."

Before the man can ask what she said, he gives a surprised cry and a small rock tumbles away from him.

"Ey! Who threw that!" he shouts to a few people, talking among themselves. They all look at the patrolman blankly. Getting no answers, the man continues his escort, muttering something about getting no respect for all his hard work.

Pulling the girls to another intersection, the man demands, "Well, where- Ah!" another rock tumbles around their feet as the man rubs his neck shouting, "Oi! Who the bloomin'-"

"I saw him, I saw him!" Twinkaleni squeaks, pointing, "A rather sinister looking man just ducked around there!"

"You runts stay put or it's the stocks for ya both!" he shouts, drawing his club to dash after the phantom rock thrower.

"Now's our chance," says Alice, and the girls

escape while trying not to *look* like they were escaping.

They walk swiftly and purposefully for a time until they feel safe enough to begin asking for directions once more. Evening is fast approaching and they desperately want to at least locate the Order's academy before it becomes dark. Fortunately, the people here seem more interested in talking while they head home for the day, at least once they realize the pair aren't asking for handouts. The girls try to make their questioning of the locals appear as if they have business there whenever patrols are present.

Nearly sundown now, the pair have followed dozens of people's directions to an isolated road of well worn stone. Twinkaleni stops upon seeing a cube like structure reaching into the darkening sky, "We're here."

The pair keep their distance, hidden, observing their first obstacles. The academy is surrounded by a high, stone wall. The only visible entrance is a portcullis, it's steel gate down for the night. Even then, there is a guard on the inside beside a lit brazier. Having planned for this, the girls remain in their hiding spot until true dark, watching and waiting. The guard wanders around some but for the most part seems intent on waiting by the gate. Twinkaleni and Alice skirt around the wall to where overgrown bushes can conceal them. Twinkaleni then uses her Earth magic to remove the gravity imposed on Alice, allowing her to easily scale the wall. Nearly weightless, the fox girl holds onto the top and peers over the wall to find the imposing, geometric academy building has a fairly large yard around it. The yard has only a little brush but is otherwise clear, allowing for Alice to see there are no other guards but also that the girls will have little cover when they attempt to cross.

The top of the wall has strange little spires poking up from it every few feet. In the dark, Alice can't make out details but feels they will be strong enough to hold their weight, her own returning to her. She ties a rope to one. The wall is an impressive two feet or so thick, and Alice hooks her legs around one of the smooth metal spires so she can pull up Twinkaleni, now hanging onto the other end of the rope. Once the Murin is up, she takes a look around before the two descend into the academy grounds.

Darkly cloaked, the girls swiftly make their way

around the massive building, avoiding the main entrance entirely as they had planned. The walls to the academy building are sheer and smooth, curiously so. Alice had never seen such a structure. There are a couple of side doors but Twinkaleni is sure they will be locked, as well as a few unlit gazebo like structures. Eventually, they come across a section of wall with particularly large windows perhaps a full story off the ground and two more tall.

"We are, in luck," huffs Twinkaleni, "The windows, remain open." The mage had said during their planning that these enormous windows would be their best chance at a stealthy entry, as they often stand open, even in late summer, to help cool and light the academy's library.

No light emanates from within and so, as before, Twinkaleni levitates Alice up to the window sill. Alice spreads her body and holds onto the thick, wooden frame of the massive mosaic windows with one hand, looking around inside. All she can see are the silhouettes of things, and only them because of some distant and obscured light source. Instead, she listens for a time, her triangular fox hear angling around for any sound. Hearing nothing, she climbs onto the sill, freezing once more to listen. Again, there are no sounds though her anxiety steadily rises. Outside, they could still flee, lose themselves in the city and break for the safety of the forest, but once inside, there would be little chance of escape, and harsh punishment for intruders.

The moon light shows Alice that the windows are a ways up from the floor, perhaps six feet or more. The fox girl positions herself between two book shelves and dangles from the window sill, dropping as silently as she can to the floor. She then ties the last two of her ropes together in the hopes it will be long enough to reach Twinkaleni and tosses one end out the window. Looking around in the near complete darkness for something to anchor the rope to, Alice decides she would be the best choice not to make any sound and ties the rope around her waist. When she feels Twinkaleni give a few tugs on the other end, Alice pulls the Murin up, pausing with every tiny sound she makes to listen for any disturbances. When Twinkaleni scrambles onto the window sill she looks around for a way down. Alice reaches up to her and the Murin nods, leaping into the fox girl's arms. They were in.

The library smells like old dust and other things

Alice doesn't recognize. Either Twinkaleni can see better in the dark or remembers her way around because she is able to lead them down an isle with little difficultly. The walls and isles are lined with shelves of varying heights, all considerably taller than Alice. If these shelves were packed with books as they appeared to be, this room had more literature than Alice thought existed in the whole world.

The pair creeps down a main isle, slowing as they close in on a small light, not on a wall like Alice had thought, but coming from one of the isles. Heart racing, Alice peers around a bookshelf down the isle to see the light is coming from a candle set on a low shelf. There is a person sitting beside it, back against the shelf, reading from a tome that takes up their entire lap. Twinkaleni looks to Alice, points to herself and makes a talking gesture. Alice takes it to mean she wishes to make contact. The Murin mage soundlessly makes her way down the isle, Alice following, until she is just at the edge of illumination.

Alice recognizes the person as a young Tokala like herself. So immersed are they in reading that they don't even look up when Twinkaleni steps into the candle light. They do however jump enough to slap the book closed when Twinkaleni whispers, "Justin."

He jumps again when he spots the pair. "Who, who are you?" he asks in a cracking boy's voice.

"Justin, it is I, Twinkaleni Orbear. Do you remember me?" asks Twinkaleni, getting a little closer.

The boy scoots back on his bottom, tossing back, "If you wish me harm, you will not find me easy prey. Kiho!"

With the word, the boy puts his hands before him as if caught mid clap. The air dries suddenly and the boy vanishes in a cloud of misty, cool fog. The candle is blown out from within the fog just as Twinkaleni squeaks, "Get him!"

Alice charges forth, the fog already clearing. She can hear the boy's panicked movements as he makes for the other end of the isle and Alice flashes forward, fear of discovery lending her speed. She trips over what turns out to be the hem of the boy's robes and they both go tumbling nosily to the ground. Alice manages to straddle the boy before he can rise and clamps a hand over his muzzle, the blade of a bone knife at his throat.

"We're not here to hurt you but move and you're dead," Alice whispers hoarsely into the boy's face, his body going rigid under her. He looks up at her in wide eyed horror and then to Twinkaleni as she approaches.

They wait, unmoving for a minute to listen for any signs of alarm, but the rest of the library remains still and silent. The Murin mage conjures a grain sized speck of light bright enough only to show their three faces.

"That was unnecessary," whispers Twinkaleni, removing the hood of her cloak, "We mean you no harm. Do you not remember me? It has been a few years but we once studied the art together."

The boy, Justin, looks to Twinkaleni in surprise. Perhaps exposing her great ears has jogged some memory loose because he mumbles something through Alice's hand, more curious than alarmed.

"You recall me then?" Twinkaleni asks. The boy

gives a quick nod. Twinkaleni grins, "I am glad of that. We only wish to talk. But be forewarned, my companion can kill you five times in five ways before you could even draw a breath. So I advise you not to call out."

Alice does her best to look the part of such an assassin, giving the boy what she hopes is a cold, steely gaze. The boy looks to her and then nods once more. She uncovers his mouth. He watches Alice warily for a moment, not even blinking, which makes Alice want to smile though she suppresses it.

"It's good to see you again, Justin," says Twinkaleni, taking the boy's attention.

"Twinkaleni?" he shakes his head in disbelief, "How can this be? I thought you dead long ago."

Twinkaleni frowns, "Dead? Hardly. I escaped. I've been living free in the world outside these walls all this time."

"The masters. They said you had succumbed to demonic possession and rampaged into the city. They said you killed many innocent people until an enraged mob tore you to pieces," Justin recounts.

"More lies told by the Order to keep us under control," insists Twinkaleni, "The world is not at all what they say. *We* are not at all what they say. I have lived in the real world. People do not fear us as the demon spawn the masters have told us we are. Our abilities can be celebrated and sought assets to those we aid."

"Our powers are the result of demonic corruption. We can only be purified through service to the Thermathrogi," claims Justin.

"It's true. Twinkaleni isn't a demon, and neither are you. Her magic can be beautiful and amazing. She's saved my life more times than I can count with it," counters Alice.

The boy looks to Alice curiously, "Who are you?"

"This is Alice, a dear friend," explains Twinkaleni, the boy looking to her in surprise, "Yes, I have made friends in the outside world. They have risked their lives in aiding my escape from the clutches of the Order, and they aid me still in this. I have lived beyond the Order of Thermathrogi's reach and have come to know this place for what it is. A prison. A prison meant to break us, to pervert our will, to use our gifts to further their own goals, to force us into perpetual servitude through lies and cruelty. The Order will never release us, service or no. We are tools to them, too valuable to let go. That is why I have returned. To free us all from the Order's chains."

"The Order protects us within these walls," asserts the fox boy, "They train us so we may serve. We serve to prove ourselves loyal so that we may live lives of worth and value, for the greater good of Arsalia."

"Protect us from whom? Those that the Order claims tore me apart? That I even stand before you is proof of the Order's lies," exclaims Twinkaleni, her tiny light's strength rising, showing that Justin's fur is pale, perhaps tan or white, marbled with darker streaks.

"You could be a demon, using this form to tempt me. This could all be some test," Justin says, looking to Alice.

"I'm not a demon," Alice practically snarls.

Twinkaleni only sighs, "I suppose, in essence, it is a test. A test to see who would fight for their freedom so they may live by their own terms, and who would yield it, to be kept in a cage, fed on lies until unleashed on your master's enemies like some mindless war beast. I will not force you to accept my words. Alice, let him up please."

Alice moves to stand beside the Murin, sheathing her knife but ready to move on the boy if he tries anything. Justin looks warily at the two of them before rising to a sit. He then asks, "If what you say is true, and I'm not implying at all that it is, how did you escape?"

And so Twinkaleni tells her story starting with her last days at the academy.

A lesson had the young mage's in training pair up and take turns exchanging magical blows while their partners defused them. In the Order, students were allowed to proceed to more advanced lessons only after proving their mastery with their current. In their rush to have battle ready mages, the Order punished those who took too long to achieve this mastery. If after a mage still did not improve, they were removed. Any that were removed were never heard from again. This gave the magelings extra incentive to constantly strive to excel.

During the exercise, Twinkaleni had noticed that there were more masters observing than usual. This generally meant they were looking for candidates worthy to progress in their studies. Taught to desire little else other than mastery over their powers so they may offer them in service to Arsalia, a young Twinkaleni, being very small and having done little of note, was frequently overlooked for advancement. She wanted very much to catch the attending masters' attention. When it was her turn, she struck her partner with all her might, overcoming the young mage's defenses and burning him severely. Justin recalls this as well. He recounts how the masters praised her for this display of power, even over the tortured screams of the scorched child. It helped that Twinkaleni's partner was seen as a sort of quickly ascending protege and she coming near to removal. The Murin mage had never felt worse for being born with the touch of magic.

During her continued studies, Twinkaleni did all she could to help the young boy she had so recklessly ruined, going well out of her way to insure he made it to lessons on time, helping him practice, and even bringing him food when he was unable to manage himself. Though despite her efforts the boy was eventually removed. The masters would never say what exactly happened to students who had been removed, only that they would no longer be taking part in lessons.

Removed students simply seemed to vanish overnight along with their belongings, leaving only questions as evidence they existed at all. With the terrible things the masters would tell the young magi awaited the unprepared in the outside world and the rumors and speculation of what really happened, it was widely believed that removal assured a truly horrible end. With so great a weight burdening her adolescent mind, Twinkaleni's performance began to slip.

The young mage found that she could no longer focus on her lessons, which led her to thoughts of her own removal, which in turn strained her focus even more. This did not go unnoticed by her masters. When told she would be facing removal herself if her performance did not improve, Twinkaleni knew she would have to flee from the

Order, risking the dangers of an unknown world to the certainty of brutal punishment dealt by the masters of Thermathrogi.

One night, when all were asleep, Twinkaleni made her escape. At first she attempted to squeeze through the opening's in the main portcullis' gate, thinking her uniquely small frame could manage it. But the moment she touched the steel, she was struck by some energy that flung her away. The enchantment on the gate also made a loud pop that alerted the guards to the Murin's presence. Immediately, the spires along the outer wall began to glow with charging power. The guards closing on her and knowing she would not be given another chance, the young mage made quick calculations, angled herself, and then gathered all the air she could, flinging it at the ground at her feet.

The tiny mage launched herself clear over the wall just before the academy's barrier could fully activate. Jubilation peaked over her fear for only a split second before the rising barrier cleaved off her once long tail trailing behind her. The airborne Twinkaleni crashed into a tree along the outer wall. Hurt and near unconscious from her use of so much magic, Twinkaleni waited in the tree, her minuscule stature allowing her to hide among branches thought too weak to hold anyone as the area was searched. Figuring she had fled the moment she was outside the walls, most of the Order's agents moved on quickly to begin scouring the city.

After a moment to gather herself, Twinkaleni left the tree, knowing it would not be long before the Order had devices made from her severed tail to track her. Driven by desperation, pain, and fear, she made it out of Klepor and had been on the run ever since.

While Twinkaleni continues her tale, Alice looks around the library some, having heard it before. She had never been in a library, or even seen one for that matter. Its stale, musty scent hid vast amounts of knowledge, Alice was sure. The guide she had bought for Twinkaleni so long ago was the single most expensive thing she had ever purchased and it had helped them tremendously. Alice can only imagine the secrets the countless tombs on these shelves held within their pages. Alice could read some, but in the darkness, could see only see a few titles. Most looked like histories. There are ladders on small wheels leaning against the shelves, granting access to the higher levels. Alice is looking at one when she sees Justin staring at her. He turns away the moment she notices, but during Twinkaleni's story, she catches him looking her way quite a few times.

Not one to shy from a thorough explanation, Twinkaleni goes on for what feels like hours. It didn't help that Justin wanted details on Twinkaleni's various new spells, which she was only too happy to oblige. Alice mostly listens, Justin asking her questions, mostly about her part in the story as if to validate it. Alice wasn't one to reveal so much of herself to a stranger and keeps her responses simple and concise, though she does show the boy Jellybane when Twinkaleni gets to it. The fox mage can feel the enchantment as Twinkaleni can and admits such complex magic would be difficult to have managed by other means. They also show him the enchanted red cloak of the Order as proof of their hard won victory over one of their terrible agents.

Twinkaleni is about where the girls had met Kaliska when, yawning, Alice notices it's getting a little easier to see. This is because morning is quickly approaching.

"Oh ticks, we gotta go," says Alice, nudging Twinkaleni and pointing out the library's great windows.

The Murin mage squeaks, "I've completely lost track of time, we must hurry."

As the girls prepare to depart, Justin follows them calling, "Wait, will you be returning?"

Twinkaleni says back to him, "That depends. Will you do all you can to prevent the masters hearing any of this?"

"Yes, yes of course," Justin assures.

"Then we will return in a week's time, here in the library," says Twinkaleni as Alice climbs up the rope and onto the sill.

"You as well?" Justin asks up to Alice.

"Uh, yeah," Alice says, pulling Twinkaleni up along with her rope. Justin grins at this and hurries off.

Chapter 7

Magi

Alice and Twinkaleni manage to leave Klepor without incident to meet back with Danahlia and Squiggles in the forest. Twinkaleni is ecstatic about the mission's success, not only gaining entry into the academy but also making contact with the mages. It was a rather harrowing experience for Alice, sneaking about under the Order's nose, but worthwhile just to see the joy on the small mouse girl's face and the bounce in her step. Her large ears flap like wings as she skips along, going on and on about how their first mission had exceeded all her expectations and all she hopes to accomplish in future ones.

When they reach the forest, the pair follow the tracking device Twinkaleni had devised and eventually find Danahlia with Squiggles. The moment the Liguna spots them, she races over and grabs them both in a powerful hug.

"Ticks and fleas, I was so worried about you guys!" Danahlia exclaims, squeezing hard and giving

Alice a kiss on the cheek and Twinkaleni one on her forehead.

Twinkaleni starts to squirm as she tries to tell the Liguna of the mission, but Danahlia squeezes harder saying, "Nope, not yet." Squiggles makes his happy throaty grumbles at the reunion and snuffles around at them before pushing his muzzle in between the embracing girls and giving them licks. After a minute Danahlia still doesn't release them, but asks, "Ok, so how did it go?"

Twinkaleni wiggles free and begins to pace excitedly, telling Danahlia of their success while Alice let's herself be held for a good while longer. Danahlia had managed to catch something that was brown and furry, and now cooks over a small fire. Squiggles must be doing well too while the cold blooded pair hide, as he shows little interest in it.

After a few days' rest, Twinkaleni and Alice make the long walk back to Klepor to be in time for their next meeting with Justin. The pair once more sneak into the Order academy library but instead of one mage waiting for them, there are three. It seems the fox mage could not contain the news of Alice and Twinkaleni's visit and has told his friends.

Along with Justin are Parnella, an Urock girl, and Clifford, a Houndain boy, both around the same age as Alice. The girls spend about as much time telling the rest of their story as they do answering the trio's curious questions and before they know it, it's time for Alice and Twinkaleni to make their escape once more.

Over a series of weeks, Alice and Twinkaleni are met by a slowly increasing number of magi, curious about their weekly visitors. On their latest meeting, Rosie, an older Echanian girl, has in her arms an especially young Didel, little more than a toddler. Many of the others have come only to see if what Justin and his friends have said was true and have not committed to openly defying the Order yet, though all promise to keep the meetings a secret. In the very back corner of the library, Twinkaleni is giving them her hushed speech about freedom, the atrocity and hypocrisy that the Order is committing by imprisoning and lying to them by claiming it is for their safety only to be using them as weapons, when the tiny opossum girl tugs on Alice's cloak saying in a quavering voice, "I wanna go home."

Rosie holds her a little tighter, whispering, "I

know, Allie. Soon. We have to wait a little longer first."

Twinkaleni tries to continue but Allie presses, "I want my momma." Her voice carrying in the silent library.

Rosie pets the girl, trying to calm her, "Shh, soon."

Though Twinkaleni had told her of how the Order takes even the youngest children with a hint of magical talent, Alice had trouble believing it until now. Allie had only recently been plucked from her parents arms and taken to be processed by the Order of Thermathrogi into a new instrument of war. The magi tell her it was actually quite common, even preferred by the Order, to get them so young, before they developed strong memories and attachments to their families. This made it easier to indoctrinate them according to Twinkaleni.

Alice takes the girl by the hand, assuring, "We'll get you home, we'll get you all home."

"Alice, you know it will not be so simple," Twinkaleni reminds.

Then Rosie asks, "Can't you just take Allie? I thought you were planning on rescuing us. Take Allie now, get her back to her parents. You can come back for us later once more have agreed to leave."

Twinkaleni shakes her head, "I'm afraid that is not possible. The moment one of you is reported missing the Order will no doubt bolster security, making reentry considerably more difficult if not impossible. The risk to everyone will be too great then. We must all escape together or likely none will leave this place." She then addresses the others, "Even if you were to escape with us, it is unlikely you will be able to see your families for some time." After a few troubled looks and whys, Twinkaleni says, "Consider your parents will be the first to be questioned should you leave the Order. It is unclear what may happen to them, but to insure their safety, it would be best if they had no knowledge of your whereabouts. Make no mistake, escape from the Order will only be the beginning of our struggle. It may be lifetimes before we are truly free from those who would enslave our powers for their own desires."

Alice can see frowns deepening in the

gathered children's faces, even by Twinkaleni's dim light, as this sinks in. Allie whines pitifully in Rosie's arms, "I wanna go home."

Clifford asks, "So even if we leave, we won't be able to go see our families?"

"It would be unsafe to do so at first," answers Twinkaleni, "But in time, once we've established a safe haven, perhaps we could all bring our families to live with us, somewhere far from the Order's reach."

"But where?" asks Parnella.

"The Wildlands beyond the Gadara mountains," says Twinkaleni.

"That's so far," says Rosie, some of the others making similar comments.

"We have friends in the mountains that will help," assures Alice, "If you can make it that far, you should be safe."

"And from there we will seek new lives of freedom beyond Arsalia's borders," affirms

Twinkaleni.

"Allie couldn't walk that far, most of the younger ones couldn't either, and with the Order on our tails..." Rosie trails off.

Twinkaleni raises her hands to the groups concerns over such a trek, "We will not have to walk the entire way, indeed, not even most of it. We have a dragon."

The Murin mage outlines her plan of using Squiggles to ferry the fleeing mages to the girl's camp in the mountains, where they will learn to live off the land as she and Alice had. Once they have some experience, they will move on into the Wildlands. With the Gadara mountains forming an imposing natural barrier, nearly impassable to those who do not know the caves that go through them, Twinkaleni is certain they will be safe to begin a community free of oppression and servitude for the magically gifted.

The plan is generally well received though some doubt Squiggles' existence, citing that dragons have been extinct for a very long time. Twinkaleni produces a few of Squiggles old scales and teeth as evidence. The mage children handle them in awe though some remain skeptical. Twinkaleni and Alice are telling the young magi of their dragon's origin when an adult female voice startles them all.

"Just *what* is going on here?" demands a Feladine woman of middle years in a deep red robe. She holds something in her palm that lights the darkness around her with the strength and color of a camp fire. Everyone jumps and Twinkaleni's light goes out. "And *who* are you two?"

"Master Felenius," blurts Rosie, "Uh, we couldn't sleep, so..."

"Yeah," agrees Clifford, "Allie was crying again."

Master Felenius raises a brow, "Who?"

"Apprentice Alivia," provides Parnella, pointing to the tiny opossum girl.

"Ah yes, our newest inductee. Tell me child, why are you crying?" asks the robed cat woman.

Allie sniffles, "I wanna go home."

"Oh but you are home," says Master Felenius gesturing around, "This is your home now, and we are your family. Isn't it nice having so many brothers and sisters?"

Allie frowns, "I want momma."

Master Felenius' mouth becomes a line, "Now we will have none of that. How can you be so selfish? The Order of Thermathrogi has taken you in from a heartless world, fed you, clothed you, and we will teach you to be a very valuable person. You will do well to show respect."

"She's still getting used to things, Master Felenius," says Rosie before the woman can say more, "I'll make sure she knows how good she has it here, and how much the Order is doing for us all. This is only a phase and won't last long."

"Be sure that it does not," huffs Master Felenius, "The rest of you need to be in bed. I know you are all eager to learn, but this is unacceptable. If you have so much energy, I expect each of you would enjoy reporting to me after supper tomorrow for extra lessons. Any one of the other Masters would have you all spend a day or two in the box for such a breach. Now go, off with you."

The others immediately prepare to depart with a unified, "Yes, Master Felenius," some even adding a thank you. Alice and Twinkaleni follow suite until the cat woman's eyes fall upon them.

"And who might you two be?" she asks, her feline eyes narrowing.

"They just came from Boreadon with the others," says Justin.

Master Felenius nods, "Oh yes, the transfers."

"Mm-hm, they don't quite know their way around yet. I'll get 'em to their bunks, Master." says Justin, waving a hand to the pair.

Heart pounding, Alice can feel the Feladine woman's eyes boring into her as she passes, saying, "Be sure that you do. And know this kind of behavior is not tolerated here."

"Yes, Master," Alice and Twinkaleni say dutifully as they leave the library and enter a stone hallway sparsely lit by glowing stones. Alice can't help but look back to find the robed Feladine watching them as they go but at least not following.

Justin leads them around a corner and lets out a breath, "Ticks, that was close."

"I can't believe them, saying they're your family?" spits Alice.

"Now is not the time to discuss it, we must depart before rousing further suspicion," says Twinkaleni.

"Yeah, if you go down this hall," Justin points the way they were going, "and keep making lefts at the intersections, you'll circle back to the library."

"I remember," says Twinkaleni making her way down the hall, Alice following.

They proceed carefully to sneak back into the library, finding Master Felenius crouched down with her magical light source where the group had met. She's examining something she found on the floor but Alice and Twinkaleni focus on getting out of the building rather than paying much attention to the woman's activities. As quietly as they can,

Twinkaleni levitates Alice up to the window sill and Alice in turn pulls up the Murin on their rope. They do the same at the outer wall and are in the city before allowing themselves to relax and breathe. They had been fortunate that Alice suggested they acquire cloaks similar to the young magi just in case such an event had occurred. For now, they head back to Danahlia and Squiggles.

During their next week's visits, several of the young mages agree to leave the Order and seek out a life of freedom. Not as many as Twinkaleni had hoped, the majority still fearing their masters' wrath, but she says any would have made their efforts worthwhile. Justin, Parnella, Clifford, Rosie, and little Allie are among those who wish to leave and plans are made for their departure. A week later, the girls execute their final infiltration of Klepor's Order academy. Danahlia and Squiggles are set to wait much closer to the city so they may quickly fly in and pick up the escaping magi before zipping back out in an effort to rouse the least attention. As Alice and Twinkaleni make their way over the outer wall for the last time, Twinkaleni sends up a small but bright ball of starlight into the air where it quickly disappears among the stars in the clear night sky. This was to signal Danahlia and

Squiggles to make their approach.

When Alice and Twinkaleni climb in through the library's window sill, Alice's fur bristles. Something is off. She places a stopping hand on Twinkaleni's shoulder, lowering the hood of her robe to sniff the air while angling her ears in an effort to understand her unease. Generally, one of the mage children would be watching for their arrival to greet them. No one came tonight but that was not unusual, sometimes the others would be too deep in discussion to notice. It was quite too. Often the pair could hear the children excitedly whispering among themselves at least, though on this night they could just be waiting patiently in the dark for their chance to escape. But then why no greeters?

Twinkaleni takes Alice's lead and looks around, lowering her own hood, her large round ears perked. Nothing. The Murin then waves the fox girl on and hurries for the back corner where the mages meet. Alice follows, looking into the deeply shadowed room for anything amiss. She hears Twinkaleni calling quietly to the young magi but none answer.

"Perhaps something has kept them. We may

have to wait," says Twinkaleni searching around.

"I don't like this. I think we should go. We can try again later," Alice urges.

"Oh, there will not be a later," a man's voice echoes from somewhere in the dark room.

Other voices from all around call, "Ahlok." Alice and Twinkaleni freeze when several sources of illumination burst into being. As Alice's eyes adjust to the suddenly bright room, she looks to find three robed figures all flanked by two guards armed with capped staves blocking each isle, trapping her and Twinkaleni in the corner. The robed figures each hold out a hand, the sources of light in their palms.

One of the hooded figures steps forth, pulling back it's hood to reveal an elderly Leonain with a heavily grayed mane, trimmed to give him angular features. He grins, revealing sharp teeth, and speaks with strength despite his years, "Apprentice Twinkaleni Orbear. At long last our wayward daughter returns." He looks to Alice, "And you even brought me a gift as recompense for your misdeeds. Tell me, is the Tokala of potential value to the Thermathrogi, or is she simply a plea for forgiveness?"

"Grand Master Balk," Twinkaleni whispers, her eyes lowering to the ground.

"ANSWER ME!" Balk roars, causing the frightened girls to jump and shiver. When Twinkaleni is unable to respond, the elderly lion man shakes his head, saying in a defeated tone, "Like any father, I expect great things from my children. For all I give all I ask is obedience." After a pause he continues, "Why is it that you insist on hurting your father? Why is it that you desire to turn my children against me?"

Alice sees Twinkaleni's tiny hands become shaking fists. Balk looks like he's going to roar again but Twinkaleni beats him to it, her generally small squeaky voice gaining strength and depth with each word, "You, are not, my, father. And we, are not, your, children."

"Such insolence. Perhaps a year, no, two years in a box will give you the time necessary to reflect on your poor judgment," Balk sneers, then commands, "Restrain this impudent mageling. Kill the oth-"

Before he can finish, Twinkaleni shouts, "Asendiote!" with a raise of her hands. The air around Alice attempts to lift her for a second and the robed figures' lights fly up from their open palms, losing their power and plunging the library back into darkness.

"Get them, NOW! Activate the diffuser and raise the damned barrier!" Balk shouts from the shadows as his people call in confusion.

The darkness is less hindering to Alice and Twinkaleni, having been through the dark library many times already. Alice reaches to free Jellybane from the sheath at her back but her robe hides the handle. One of the guard's silhouettes is approaching quickly and Alice scrambles to pull off her robe, tossing it over the man. As he struggles with it, she pulls free her sword and whispers to Twinkaleni, "We gotta get outta here."

"No," Twinkaleni harshly spits back, Balk demanding light, "We must free the others or all will be for not."

"Twinkaleni, we-" Alice slashes at what might

be the hand of the cloak covered guard causing the man to scream. She then grabs Twinkaleni's robe and tugs her toward toward the isle leading to the windows while stepping around the screaming man. Others close in quickly from all directions.

"No!" Twinkaleni growls, pulling free. The mage extends her small pink hands out to her sides and thunders, "Vespis Flomino!"

With a gigantic whoosh, the air around Alice suddenly parts with such force that for a split second it feels like her arms and legs are going to be pulled off. She only has time to blink and gasp as screaming echoes in the dark room and flailing shapes are sent flying away. Massive shelves grown and bang, toppling over each other, their payload of books falling to the floor like the guts of eviscerated animals.

The wind attack leaves only a few of the Order's agents standing, most taking cover as Twinkaleni draws her miniature weapons. "We can take them!" she assures Alice.

"Twinkaleni! I didn't come here to kill people!" Alice shouts over the ringing in her ears.

The Murin mage points negligently over to the windows with her needle-like blade, "Then go! Pray your spared enemies do not seek vengeance!" She swipes her sword before her shouting "Vespis Flowmino!" once more.

A burst of wind, not as powerful as the first, slams into the shins of the guard charging at her with raised staff. The man's legs shoot back behind him and he falls forward hard. Before he can react, Twinkaleni ruthlessly thrusts her rapier deep into his eye. Finding his brain, she gives her wrist a little swirl before swiftly retracting it and moving on to another.

The look of horror on the man's face as Twinkaleni ended his life has Alice standing frozen. She did not want to be a murderer, someone who so carelessly ends another person's life, but by running away she would be abandoning her friend, likely resulting in the mouse girl's own death. Alice notices those knocked away by Twinkaleni's initial blast recovering. She sees this because the room was getting a little brighter, not by the morning sun but by some faint glow coming from high up along the library walls. The room has a strange strip of unknown material outlining it just below the ceiling that emanates the slightest brown light. She also feels more then hears a hum in the air that strengthens with the earth colored glow.

Twinkaleni finishes another guard and even one of the robed figures with a combination of magic and sword play but looks to be struggling more than exhaustion would merit. A pompous roar of laughter echoes from somewhere in the vast room and Balk mocks, "How gifted a killer you've become my delinquent daughter! Your father is so very proud of you! But even all these gifts of blood will not negate your punishment! You forget who the real master of your power is in these walls!"

The remaining robed figures are finding their enchanted light sources, revealing the girls more to them and their guards. One of the masters lifts a ringed finger to Alice spitting, "Rairak!"

Remembering their last encounter with an agent of the Order, Alice knows this is not a good situation to be in. She leaps behind a fallen pair of bookshelves just before the ring glows blue, erupting with a vicious arc of azure lighting that scorches the thick red rug Alice had just been standing on, burning a hole to the stone floor. Alice peaks over the shelves and the robed Master repeats the harsh word, unleashing another bolt that the fox girl just barely ducks under. While pinned, Alice sees a guard coming around to her side and begins desperately hurling fallen books at him. The guard blocks some with his staff but enough of the heavy tomes get through to keep him at bay until a familiar heavy flapping takes everyone's attention.

The flapping gets steadily louder and soon Squiggles can be seen outside the library's great windows as he circles the building low to the ground before landing. Alice hears Danahlia calling from atop him, "Guys! You in there?!"

Most of the guards and robbed figures wander over to the windows, completely mesmerized at the sight of a dragon. They jump back, some nearest the windows even falling backward with startled shouts when Squiggles sticks his enormous head in to make his own inspection. He looks over the room until he finds Alice, making a happy grumble at his discovery.

"Squigs!" Alice shouts, pointing to the Order's personnel by the windows, "Infermious!"

The dragon turns his huge head to the stunned masters and their guards before a deep roar bathes them in flame. Over their screams, Alice hears Danahlia calling her name. As the wooden shelves and their many paper books rapidly catch fire, Alice spots Danahlia peeking in through the window, climbing up Squiggle's neck.

"Alice! What's goin' on?! Where's Twinkie?!" the Liguna shouts.

In her own battle, Alice had lost track of the mage and looks around in the growing inferno for her. More guards and robed masters arrive but are kept back by the raging flames quickly consuming the library. Alice spots Twinkaleni making her way toward Balk. The aged lion man looks to be in a great deal of pain, held on his knees by Twinkaleni's magic. The Murin mage herself approaches him slowly, but more out of a desperate effort than any interest in prolonging the man's suffering. Her eyes glow furiously gold, one hand extended toward the prostrate man while the other loosely holds her rapier. Her steps slow even more with each she takes. Then, only feet from her target, her legs give out and she stumbles, falling to the ground.

Thinking she wounded, Alice makes her way to the Murin mage, avoiding the fire as best she can while calling to her. Something takes hold of Alice's ankle. Startled, she looks to find a guard, half trapped under a burning bookcase, grabbing and snarling obscenities at her. Alice kicks but the man's grip is strong and he manages to pull her down. She lands hard on the stone floor, losing Jellybane. She grabs frantically for her sword, kicking at the man but his hands climb up her legs pulling her closer to him and further from her enchanted weapon.

As his grasping hands reach her thighs, Alice pulls free her bone bladed knife and stabs wildly at the man's arms, causing him to recoil and scream, warm blood sprinkling over her. She kicks free of him, recovering her sword to find Twinkaleni struggling just to remain on her hands and knees. Balk stands over her, the Murin's mini rapier looking especially small in his large hands.

"Twinkaleni!" Alice cries, racing for her.

At the same time she hears Danahlia shout from the window, "Adarath!"

A great heat forces Alice to turn away, a boulder of fire streaking past her, clipping the lion man and bursting into the wall beyond him. Balk is sent flailing back only to be knocked forward again by the fireball's explosion, his robes catching. Twinkaleni is sent flying into an empty portion of bookshelf, sparing her the fiery bolt's detonation, but the shelf is burning, it's remaining books leading hungry flames right to the unmoving Murin.

Alice makes her way as quickly as she can to Twinkaleni, Danahlia shouting to them, "That was a bad guy, right?"

Alice sheathes her sword, taking up the mouse girl and pulling her from the burning shelf. As she adjusts her hold on the small mage, she hears another harsh cry of, "Rairak!"

Alice instinctively ducks, nearly loosing Twinkaleni, as a bolt of lighting arcs over her. Danahlia shouts "Adarath!" in reply, sending a fireball at the gathering of masters and guards blocked by fire near the library's main entrance. Alice keeps low, half carrying and half dragging the nearly unconscious Murin in her effort to escape the burning building while trying to avoid a direct line of sight with the robed lighting throwers. The heat and smoke in the library become intense and Alice struggles even with the Murin's relatively light weight as she coughs. Her eyes water from the smoke, obscuring her vision, but Alice drags on in the direction of the windows and their salvation.

Squiggles unleashes a hellish barrage on the Order's minions once Alice and Twinkaleni are out of direct harm as Danahlia shouts, "Hurry! Somethin's happenin' to the wall out here and it doesn't look good!"

By the time Alice has Twinkaleni near the windows, Danahlia has tied their rope around one of Squiggles' horns. Alice grips the rope, holding Twinkaleni close and Danahlia orders the dragon back. Squiggles pulls his head from the library, easily hoisting Alice and Twinkaleni up to the sill and out of the inferno. Through stinging tears, Alice can see a purplish, waving light about them. Tendrils of intense purple reach higher and higher into the air from the short spires atop the academy's outer wall. Between the tendrils rises a curtain of angrily, crackling, violet energy.

Alice coughs, "What is that?"

"The barrier. We must escape before it reaches full power," Twinkaleni moans.

"Where's everybody else?" Danahlia asks, lifting Alice and a slack Twinkaleni onto Squiggles' back.

"It was a trap. We couldn't get 'em," says Alice, holding Twinkaleni while pulling up Danahlia to sit behind her.

Once Danahlia has his reigns, she calls to Squiggles, "Fly! Fly! Get us outta here!"

The dragon rumbles and begins flapping his mighty wings as the girls watch the wild purple energy reach up around them, but not straight up. As Squiggles leaps from the ground, the magical field stretches high over them, attempting to converge into a massive dome over the entire academy.

"Oh ticks!" Danahlia cries, "Squigs! Get your scaly butt up there or no treats for a month!"

Squiggles grumbles, flapping hard as they slowly rise, but Alice can see they won't make it. The hole left at the very top of the energy field is already too small for the dragon and continues to shrink. The dragon climbs for it but roars in pain and anger when a wing grazes the field, the purple energy sizzling where it touches him. Then Alice remembers what Twinkaleni said about dragon fire burning even magic and points toward the shrinking hole shouting, "Infermious!"

Squiggles unleashes a geyser of fire at the offending field. It sizzles and pops madly against his flame but is reluctantly pushed back. The tendrils of purple energy fight to regain lost ground and Squiggles must keep up with his attack, desperately trying to widen the hole before he hits the field.

Danahlia cries, "Here it comes!" and leans over Alice.

Alice tucks in over Twinkaleni protectively as her world becomes one of intense heat, strange acrid smells, deafening sizzling pops, and bright purple lights that show even through tightly closed eyes. Then they're free in the open, cool, night air. The girls slowly relax as Squiggles roars his triumph and Alice sees the field closing under them, a corner of the Order of Thermathrogi's expansive academy in flames under the dancing tendrils of the magical barrier.

As Squiggles evens out, Danahlia shakes Alice by the arm, "You guys ok?"

Alice has gotten most of the smoke from her lungs by now and nods, feeling around Twinkaleni. "Are you hurt?" she asks the Murin. She seems shaken but otherwise intact. Alice sees her mouth move but can't hear over the wind billowing past them. "What?" Alice asks, leaning to get her ears closer to the small girl.

Twinkaleni says something but it's lost and Alice leans closer to hear the Murin repeat, "I failed them."

Alice holds the girl tighter, "No, Twinkaleni. They set a trap, you did everything you could."

Twinkaleni doesn't seem to hear her, only looking off at nothing and repeating her words, "I failed them. I failed them."

"What she say?" Danahlia calls from behind Alice.

"No, we got away. Maybe we can try again. We know more now," says Alice, not particularly liking the idea but wanting to at least try to comfort her distraught friend.

Twinkaleni suddenly looks sharply to Alice, "No, we can't. Justin, Parnella, Clifford, Rosie, and even Allie will all be severely punished, tormented, likely even killed as an example to the others, all because I failed them!" The small girl balls up a fist and begins striking the side of her own head while mumbling to herself, "I failed them. I failed them. I failed them."

"Hey, what the tick happened?!" Danahlia calls again.

Alice restrains the Murin, "Twinkaleni, stop it! We'll go back to the mountains for now. Come up with a new plan."

"NO!" Twinkaleni shouts, "We can never go back!"

Alice, still holding the tiny girl's arms, asks in surprise, "What? Why?"

"You don't understand," Twinkaleni says, defeated, "They know we have a dragon. The scales and teeth we left to the magi, the Order has them now. They may find a way to use them to track us. If we lead them back to the mountains, they will show Kaliska and the children no mercy."

"But, what are we gonna do?" asks Alice, a terrible knot forming in her gut.

"What's goin' on?!" calls Danahlia, getting impatient.

Alice does her best to explain their situation and Danahlia has Squiggles land in another forest. Quieter now, the girls discuss their predicament.

"We have to at least tell Kali. We can't just leave her to take care of the kids alone," Alice insists.

"It would be *most* unwise to take such a risk," assures Twinkaleni, "If even a single agent of the Order was left who knows our faces, they are likely to have word already spreading throughout Arsalia. I do not know what the Order might devise to track Squiggles', but going back to the mountains would surely draw them there. Vengeance upon us would spur them, but the opportunity to gain a dragon would drive the entire kingdom into a frenzy."

"As long as we have Squigs, we can go anywhere. Let's just fly far away for a while, where the Order can't touch us," suggests Danahlia.

"Where? To the Wildlands?" Alice wonders.

"I was thinking more west, like Feoria," says Danahlia.

"Feoria?" Twinkaleni blurts incredulously, "Don't be absurd. We could fly there now certainly, but what makes you think they will give Alice and I asylum? Have you forgotten there is a war between the warm and cold blooded?"

"They will 'cause I'll ask 'em," says Danahlia.

"And why would they listen to you?" Twinkaleni spits back.

Danahlia sits straighter as she announces, "Because I'm an Ashclaw."

Chapter 8

To Feoria

Alice and Twinkaleni both look blankly back at the Liguna sitting proudly behind them, chest out and head held high.

"What does that mean?" Alice asks, "What's an ash claw?"

Danahlia looks at them in disbelief, "You don't know who the Ashclaws are?"

The furred pair continue to stare.

"The Ashclaws?" Danahlia exclaims, "The greatest of hunters? The fiercest of warriors? The most beautiful of people? The Ashclaws!"

Twinkaleni sighs as Alice says, "I thought you were a Smoothide."

"Yeah, that's what I told Twinkie when we met. Just kinda rolled with it. Figured it would be safer if I came up with a clever alias."

"What use is such a name to us now?" grumbles Twinkaleni.

"Well, not that you'd know, apparently, but the Ashclaws are a very prominent Cold Blood clan. My own dad was sent as an envoy to negotiate with Arsalia to figure out what to do about all the hostility that had been rising up along the border territories. We were ambushed along the way by some nasty furbacks, no offense, and that looks like it really set off the Blood War."

"How could that be? An envoy and his family would have surely had an escort of some kind for protection. How would an angry mob of peasants overtake them so?" Twinkaleni asks thoughtfully.

"Hey! There were a lot of 'em, and not just peasants, soldiers too, armored and on horses. I saw them cut my family down," Danahlia returns hotly.

"Soldiers? Why would there..." Twinkaleni trails off.

"What? What is it?" asks Alice, confused by the new information.

"If there were soldiers involved, then this ambush was likely part of a plan, a plot to ignite a new Blood War. But why? Who would gain from such death?" wonders Twinkaleni, rubbing one of her expansive ears between two fingers.

"Who cares," says Danahlia, "If my uncle is still alive, he'll help us for sure. Then we'll have a whole army between us and the Order."

The idea greatly interests Alice. If they could take refuge in Feoria, she may be able to see if her father was really imprisoned there. "I think we should go," she says.

"You wish to entrust our lives to an 'if''?" asks Twinkaleni.

"No worries, my uncle is the chief, the whole tribe would die for him if it came to it. He'll be there," Danahlia assures her companions.

Course decided, the girls take to the air once more. Their destination, the cold blood nation of Feoria.

For what feels to Alice like forever, the trio travel west, hopping from forest to forest as they did on their way to Klepor, though this time keeping their distance from settlements. They fly only by night and spend much of their sunlit hours among the trees in search of food and water, their supply having run out some time ago. It is a real challenge to keep themselves and a dragon from hunger and thirst in these unknown lands. This is only compounded by their lack of rest, causing tempers to easily flare.

They're flying low over yet another forest, though from the air and in the dark, they all look the same. Vast expanses of formless black occasionally marked with a lighter splotch. A clearing that just might have water. Exhausted, Alice holds a napping Twinkaleni in one hand and Squiggles' reigns in the other as she scans the forest canopy. The swiftly passing air makes it even harder to see but the sun is preparing to rise, coating the world in grays of steadily lighter hues, meaning they will have to land soon. Finally, Alice spots a tiny glimmer and presses the heel of one foot along the side of Squiggles' neck to get him to bank toward it.

Danahlia's head jerks off of Alice's shoulder

leaving a damp cooling spot of drool, "Wha-what's goin' on?"

"We're landin'. I think I see water," Alice calls back and then presses both heels into Squiggles' neck telling him to descend.

He does so eagerly and the girl's must brace themselves. Twinkaleni jolts awake as Squiggles carelessly smashes through tree branches in his excitement to get to water. The moment they touch down, they must race the dragon to what turns out to be a rather small pool left over by some too short rain. They squish into the mud, dunking their waterskins while pushing at Squiggles' massive head, managing to fill perhaps half of one each before the dragon drinks the pool dry. Squiggles makes irritated grumbles at his lingering thirst as the girls do what they can to quench their own.

Danahlia's lips pop free of her skin and she looks to Twinkaleni, "Ya know, that water suckin' spell would be real useful about now."

Twinkaleni rolls over to her back after drinking what she has, "I need food and rest. Go hunt something for us before the dragon scares everything away."

"Go hunt, *please*," Danahlia tosses back, taking the bow and arrows from atop Squiggles. She then gives Alice a little kick in the thigh, "Ya comin'?"

The fox girl grudgingly gets to her feet. "We'll meet back here at noon," Alice calls back to the Murin, who only gives a negligent wave in return.

The two hunters make their way through the forest, trying to keep alert for signs of game. Alice puts a slice into every few trees they pass to mark their way. Eventually they find a decent sized lizard of some sort bathing in a beam of morning sun upon a rock. Danahlia takes aim at it and fires, but the shot sails too high. The lizard doesn't notice so she fires again, but this arrow shatters on the rock, frightening the creature into running. The girls give it chase for a short distance but lose it in the thick foliage.

Breathing hard with hands on her knees, Alice exclaims, "How did you miss?! It wasn't even movin'!"

"A bug flew right in front of my face," Danahlia

throws back.

"Both times?"

"Yeah. See, it's still here," claims Danahlia, waving the bow around at nothing until she bops Alice over the head with it.

It didn't hurt much but that the Liguna would even have the audacity to hit her drives Alice into raging charge that takes both girls to the ground. The two tussel, the fox girl trying to pry the bow from Danahlia's fingers, snarling, "Give it!" while the lizard girl pushes her away and tries to keep it from her reach. Eventually, Alice bites into Danahlia's shoulder causing her to cry out and release the bow. Alice snatches it up and shoves away, getting to her feet.

Danahlia is left sitting upright, trying to look at the bite though she can't turn her head enough. "Ticks! That hurt you flea carryin' feral!" she growls.

Feeling a mix of pride and guilt, Alice smirks, picking up her sword and their few remaining arrows, "It wasn't that hard."

Danahlia shows her a few red stained fingers, "I'm bleedin'!"

Guilt over taking her, Alice sighs, approaching and crouching beside Danahlia. The Liguna recoils a bit but Alice knows it's for show and chides, "Don't be a baby."

Danahlia eyes Alice, "Don't know if I can trust you, might go feral on me again." As Alice looks over the wound, noting she left several decent teeth marks in Danahlia's smooth, brown skin, some bleeding, some not, Danahlia continues with exaggerated pomp, holding her head up high, "Ferals don't belong around *civilized* people."

"Then it's a good thing I live in the woods with *you*," Alice throws back and begins licking the wound clean. As she does she thinks of how the Liguna's blood doesn't look or taste any different from her own. She thinks how foolish it is that people hate, kill, and even have wars over a stupid thing like what kind of blood flows through someone's veins. It's not like it was a choice for anyone. And it wasn't even cold. Danahlia felt warm, just like she always did.

Alice continues licking until she stops tasting blood. She then feels Danahlia's own tongue probing around her ear. She pauses and her ear twitches involuntarily, but Danahlia probes deeper. The tip of her thick tapered tongue slides past the sensitive fluff in Alice's ear leaving a moist and not unpleasant warmth. Alice shudders, breath leaving her, when the Liguna's tongue touches the inner flesh of her ear. The fox girl has to blink rapidly, opening her eyes wide, as she is suddenly having trouble keeping them focused while Danahlia moves her tongue in little circles along Alice's inner ear. Alice's body tingles with twitchy static making her bones feel wobbly and weak with each soft breath Danahlia puffs into her ear. Danahlia holds her close, pulling Alice down with her as they come to rest on the ground.

"Uh, wu, we-wuh," Alice stutters, her thoughts already too clouded with the intense and terribly distracting sensation to form any coherence.

Danahlia laughs fiendishly, continuing to swirl her tongue in the fox girl's ear. Ever since she had discovered this weakness, the Liguna has taken great pleasure in using it to force Alice into submission. Alice tries to push away from Danahlia, but her arms don't want to respond properly, only sliding around and over the lizard girl. Even while she makes the attempt, her mind asks her why she is even trying to stop it. She has to consciously make an effort to remember why she wanted to just now but each wondrously intoxicating swirl of Danahlia's tongue erases her previous effort and she must start over from nothing. Soon even the intent to think is gone.

Alice gives in for several immensely pleasurable minutes until Danahlia stops to rub a cheek against hers. Her thoughts slowly returning to her, Alice mumbles breathlessly, "Uh, we, we should hunt."

Stroking the fox girl's fine fur, Danahlia moans, "Mmm, we should but..."

Alice rolls away when Danahlia goes for her ear again, laughing, "No no, no more of that. We need food. Be a good little Liguna and get us some breakfast." Danahlia frowns so Alice adds, "And maybe we can have some more fun after."

Danahlia doesn't move so Alice crawls over to her and starts drumming both hands on the lizard girl's belly, chanting, "Get up, get up, get up, get up."

Danahlia endures it for a moment before sweeping an arm over herself, knocking Alice's hands from under her and grabbing the fox girl before she can recover. The lizard girl wraps arms, legs, and tail around her and the pair roll, Alice squirming with a laugh caught in her throat.

"Danny!" Alice manages to gasp, before Danahlia rolls atop her planting the fox girl's face to the dirt. Danahlia sits on Alice's back and begins ruthlessly fiddling with Alice's ears, making them twitch wildly. Alice shakes her head, wiggling but unable to move from under the larger girl's weight. "Danny, stop it!" Alice cries trying desperately to keep the Liguna's fingers from tickling her ears, "I'm hungry, we need to hunt!"

Danahlia breathes into one of Alice's ears, "Do we? Looks like I already caught me some brea-oh!" Alice headbutts Danahlia in the chin causing her to jerk back and loose balance. Alice uses the opening to wiggle onto her back and get a foot against one of Danahlia's legs, shoving it out from under her. Danahlia tumbles off to the side as Alice scrambles for her sword. The Tokala draws it and has the tip pointed to Danahlia while she still rubs her chin.

Alice grins, ignoring the ache in her head, "Now, be goo-" Before she can finish a heavy weight crashes into her side, knocking the wind from her as she's slammed against the ground.

Head pounding and world spinning, for a moment she thinks it was Danahlia, but the weight still atop her isn't the warm yielding one of her friend, but the rough, hard, firm, weight of a Cold Blood man. His face is inches from hers, but even closer is the knife held just over her eyes. Alice freezes and the man wraps an earth smelling hand over her muzzle, keeping it shut.

Danahlia shouts, "Hey!" drawing Alice's attention and she sees from the corner of her eye that three more of Cold Bloods have appeared. Two are men with one woman of varying species, all dark skinned and wearing loose leather garments. They help Danahlia up and she shouts something that sounds like, "Yataie!" to the man holding Alice down. He gives the Liguna girl a glance and says something Alice doesn't understand back but doesn't budge. Danahlia says more words in her own people's tongue and the other three Cold

Bloods respond, though the one holding Alice only glares down at his captive.

Eventually, her captor seems convinced Alice is not a threat, but is still not to be trusted. She is placed against a tree, her captor standing with arms crossed close by while the other Cold Bloods converse with Danahlia. The man standing before her is lean, but not bulky, with brown rough looking skin speckled with darker tones. He looks vaguely similar to a Liguna but with a much thicker jaw and larger nostrils. His neck also carries his head more forward than up, though that may just be the way he's standing. The man watches Alice from his periphery, though seems more interested in trying to listen to the others' conversation.

The only reaction she had gotten from him so far was him pressing both her shoulders down to sit anytime she tried to rise. Ever curious about the Cold Bloods and unable to understand what is being said, Alice tries, "What's your name?"

The man glances her way once but that's all.

She tries again, pointing to herself, "I'm Alice," she then points to him, "Who are you?"

"Tamahou," he says back without looking.

"Tamahaoo? That's your name? Tamahaoo?" Alice asks.

"Ta mahau," he says more sternly.

Alice does her best to imitate the words, but this only seems to irritate him. He crouches down before Alice and places a strong hand around her muzzle, growling, "Ta," then he squeezes her jaws together saying, "Mahaou." He lets go and Alice stops talking.

After a few minutes, Danahlia excitedly comes to her side and explains that the four Cold Bloods are part of a scouting party for the Feorian army. When they saw Alice holding a sword to Danahlia, they figured she was in trouble and came to her rescue. Danahlia had told them of Alice's part in her survival in Arsalia and how they want to get to Feoria. Now they wish to take the pair back to their camp.

"But what about Twinkaleni? We should go get her and Squiggles," says Alice.

"Come on, it'll only be for a little while. We can get Twinkie after," insists Danahlia, clearly excited over seeing more of her own kind, "They said their camp isn't too far. They have food and water. We can bring some back with us for Mini-mage."

Alice considers but says, "We should get them first and go together. She'll worry if we take too long."

Danahlia continues to argue but Alice ignores her to begin searching around the trees for the cuts she left to mark their passing. Within a few minutes, Danahlia grudgingly joins her but after a time, they can't find a single cut.

"Thought you were markin' the trees," Danahlia accuses.

"I was. Then we chased that lizard *you* missed, and you hit me," Alice grumbles.

"And then *you* bit *me*," Danahlia smirks.

"And then..." Alice can't help grinning.

"Mmm, yeah, and then what happened?" asks Danahlia, a hand under her chin as if trying to recall. She looks to Alice from the corner of her eye and sticks out her tongue, giving it a wiggle. Alice looks away shyly and Danahlia presses, "Come on, we can't find the path. Twinkie still has some of your fluff. She'll find us when she wants to."

Alice gives in and they go with the Cold Bloods to their camp. As they walk, Danahlia talks with them in their tongue, occasionally feeding Alice tidbits of what they're saying but mostly forgetting to in her excitement. It appears none of them speak Arsalian, as none try to converse with the fox girl, though Alice does notice the one who had taken her to the ground before stands nearby and just behind her. Fortunately, the somewhat uncomfortable walk isn't terribly long.

The scout's camp isn't large and has only a handful more Feorians. Other than the remains of a fire in the middle, there are a few stitched together skins hanging from branches, perhaps to protect from rain. They have managed to hunt something that must have been some sort of massive turtle, it's thick, broadly spiked shell lay upside down and emptied with the meat roasting over embers or hanging from branches to keep from ferals. Regardless of what it was, the scent of it cooking is intoxicating to the hungry, young Tokala. She resists the heavy temptation to run over and tear the cooked meat from a branch where it hangs and instead lets Danahlia bring her a portion. Alice eats greedily sitting on the ground with Danahlia and the others. She is given water and focuses on refreshing herself, not much liking the looks she's getting, while Danahlia talks to her people.

The lizard girl goes on in length and seems to be telling the scouts all about her adventures with Alice, gesturing and naming her many times. The scouts steadily abandon their tasks and gather to listen to the story, laughing some and asking questions. Alice can't understand what is being said, but she can at least enjoy Danahlia's animated gestures, especially when referring to Twinkaleni and her magic or herself swinging Jellybane.

As Danahlia tells their tale, no doubt with her usual embellishments, the other Cold Bloods become more accepting of Alice. Seeing her eat so ravenously, they offer her more meat and enjoy watching her eat her fill. Still, Alice worries about Twinkaleni. True, the Murin mage has Squiggles and is powerful in her own right, but she was still young and so very small. Alice sits with a frown, thinking of how they will find their companions if she doesn't manage to find them first. While she thinks, she watches Danahlia talking and flap her arms enthusiastically. From the laughs and skeptical looks on her people's faces, Alice figures she's telling them about Squiggles, or maybe even the Cloudstalkers.

Watching Danahlia go on and on has Alice wondering about what will happen in Feoria. With only a handful of her people, Danahlia has already seemingly forgotten about Alice's very existence. What will happen when they're in a country full of them? Alice enjoyed Danahlia's company immensely and Danahlia seemed to feel the same, but what if they only spent so much time together because there were so few alternatives? Ever since they met, they had been traveling together, moving from place to place. No real time to get to know anyone else that well. But what will happen in Feoria? Danahlia will be home, with her own kind, and there will be no reason for her to leave. Alice worries over what will happen if her Liguna loses interest in her, finds someone else she'd rather spend time with, someone she has more in common with, one of her own people. Then what will happen? She'd be alone, in a country full of strangers who have been at war with her kind for years.

Alice tries to banish her darkening thoughts, knowing they are selfish, and willing herself to believe that Danahlia wouldn't do that. She had spent years in hiding deep behind enemy lines, of course she's excited to see her people, and she'll be even more so once she's among them in her own land. Alice decides she will be happy for her love, ecstatic even. And Alice wouldn't be alone, she'll have Twinkaleni, and Squiggles, AND her father, when she finds him. *Things will work out fine*, she tells herself very sternly. *Better than fine, great! Things will be great.*

Alice jolts from her inner monologue seeing Danahlia turned toward her calling, "Hey! Furface!" When Alice looks surprised back at her, Danahlia raises a brow, "You ok?"

"Uh, yeah, why?" Alice stammers.

Danahlia shrugs and waves her over, "Come on, back me up on this. They don't believe me. Squigs is at least, *at least* five hundred feet long right?"

Alice, from then on, is consulted on many things the Cold Bloods question in Danahlia's story. She decides to go with it and agrees to all of Danahlia's exaggerations and even adds to them with even greater claims and grander gestures, leaving unpleasant thoughts behind in favor of having a little fun.

Later in the afternoon, after their story is done and many of the scouts have returned to their duties, the Liguna woman stays with the girls. She tells them more about what is going on in the war and what her party is doing here, so far into Arsalian territory. She says that for the most part, the battle lines have just swayed back and forth. The Warm Bloods, having an advantage during the winter, would push forth and then the Cold Bloods would push them back during the warmer times of the year. Each side trying to find weaknesses to exploit while keeping their own hidden. The forest they were currently in is called the Vipuado. The Vipuado forest is so thick and vast that it has long been seen as an impassable barrier by both armies and has largely been ignored as a location of limited strategic value. The Cold Blood scouts are attempting to find a way through it in the hopes that Feoria may be able to establish a strong foot hold deep in Arsalia before winter, forcing the Warm Bloods to spend time and resources rooting them out.

As the Liguna woman is telling them this, one of the younger males bursts into camp with alarming news which Danahlia translates as a giant monster coming after him. He describes the creature as having two heads with strength and size enough to topple trees. Upon hearing this, the Cold Bloods arm themselves with spears and bows while taking cover among the brush. The archers climb to high branches with great agility for a better vantage point and all look in the direction the young scout had come from. Surprised none seem interested in fleeing, Alice crouches beside Danahlia and nervously nocks an arrow in her own bow, wondering what horrible monsters may call the Vipuado home.

After a few moments, Alice can hear the crack of wood and the thud of heavy steps coming closer and closer. The archers in the trees must see something because they begin firing into the forest. Their shots are answered by a fearsome but familiar roar that shakes the very air around them.

"It's Squiggles!" Alice cries as Danahlia stands, shouting to her people.

Squiggles charges out of the forest into the scout's camp, enraged by the attack. The archers hold at Danahlia's command but draw their bows as Squiggles sights one of the spearmen on the ground and immediately reaches for him with open jaws. The man falls back at the sight of so many long, sharp teeth coming for him and Alice manages to spring toward the dragon screaming, "Squigs, stop!"

Squiggles looks to Alice for a split second but the fallen man crawling away draws the dragon's attention once more. Alice must position herself before the dragon to keep him from giving chase. Squiggles roars his frustration after the fleeing man, but with Alice and Danahlia moving to block him, he doesn't pursue. Alice plucks a single arrow from Squiggles' forehead, tossing it away as she examines the wound left. The missile met his skull and didn't go deep, but he still bleeds some.

Twinkaleni pokes her head from around the dragon's neck and calls, "Alice? Danny? Are you in need of rescue?"

Once Squiggles is calmed and the Cold Bloods are assured he will not eat them, the scouts gather before the dragon, keeping a safe distance. They keep hold of their weapons as Danahlia speaks to them and slowly fear is replaced with astonishment. They watch, mouths open, as Squiggles takes the turtle meat they had hanging from branches and swallows the morsels hole. Alice manages to snatch a piece and hands it to Twinkaleni before helping the tiny girl off the great reptile. The mage then explains, with no small amount of irritation, that she had waited for the better part of the day for Alice and Danahlia to return before using what little energy she had to try to find them with her magic. Upon finding the young scout, she figured it was likely her companions managed to get captured and kept Squiggles from eating him so they might follow him back to his camp and hopefully to the missing girls.

Alice in turn explains what happened to them and in whose company they now find themselves. They don't have any time for introductions as Squiggles makes it known that he is still hungry and the scouts lead the girls and their dragon to a river nearby. It isn't a particularly large river but looks to be home to more of the enormous turtle like creatures, giving them all the opportunity to hunt and drink. An opportunity Squiggles does not hesitate to take. After a few large gulps of water, he spots the turtles' slow movements and splashes after them. The turtles retreat into their formidable, spiked shells when he approaches, but the dragon's powerful jaws, capable of crushing stone, are barely slowed.

The scouts watch in awe at his raw might before taking a turtle for themselves. Some butcher the creature while most continue to watch Squiggles hunt, listening to Danahlia talk of all the things Squiggles has defeated and eaten in the past. The scouts clean out the turtle, leaving it's inedible organs to the river's fish while filling the empty shell with it's meat before taking it back to their camp. They do not begin cooking the turtle until dusk, not wanting the smoke to give away their position. Even then the scouts keep their fire small so the turtle takes a great deal of time to cook. Those not occupied with other duties are full of questions about Squiggles, now certain he exists, which Danahlia is only too happy to answer. With Squiggles still hunting, Alice notices they take great interest in Twinkaleni as well, many watching her as if in anticipation of something.

The Murin mage notices too and eventually asks why they feel the need to stare. Danahlia then reveals that she had told her people of Twinkaleni's ability to create fire from thin air, bring rocks to life, and suck entire trees dry of their water, among other things. The scouts seem to be waiting for her to display this awesome power though Twinkaleni refuses to indulge them, saying it would be foolish and a waste of precious energy.

After hearing the scouts' disappointment, Danahlia says, "You should hear 'em, Twinkie. Throwin' all kinds o' doubt your way. Oolong says you probably can't even light a candle."

"Why would I possibly care what they think? There is no reason, no reason at all to further exhaust myself simply for their amusement," states Twinkaleni, though after a moment she asks, "Which is Oolong?"

Danahlia points to a male Cold Blood turning pieces of meat over the embers of the fire. Twinkaleni then negligently waves a hand to him, saying disinterestedly, "Feasta."

The embers suddenly burst into flames causing Oolong to jump back in surprise. He's forced to scoot further on his butt as the flames reach for him for a moment before returning to mere embers once more. After their initial shock, the others laugh at Oolong's expense. Danahlia says that there are magic wielders in Feoria too, and it is considered common sense not to anger them. Twinkaleni seems satisfied and eventually Squiggles returns to them once his belly is finally full.

The girls spend the night with the scouts and by morning both parties prepare to move on. The scouts have already spent more time than they meant to encamped and intend to travel further east while the girls continue west. It is difficult for Alice to wish them well, considering they mean to fight with her own people, so she mostly waits with Twinkaleni and Squiggles while Danahlia says her good-byes. Danahlia is in good spirits after the two groups part ways. The scouts had told her that if they just keep heading the way they are, eventually they will encounter Feoria and likely more of the Cold Blood army. She encouragingly says the army will likely know more about the possibility of Alice's father being imprisoned.

On that note, the girls and their dragon resume their journey.

Chapter 9

Ashclaw

The girls travel for days more, flying by night and hiding in the thickest forests they can find by day. Sometimes while they fly, they can see tiny orange lights on the ground. Fires to ward off the cooling night air. Occasionally there are many lights, seas of them. The girls steer clear of these rather than fly over, believing them to be army encampments. As far as they know, they're still in western Arsalia and being seen would only bring the Order of Thermathrogi's wrath on them. These flickering seas can stretch and speckle the landscape for miles, forcing the girls to make extended detours. Even so, their spirits are lifted some, believing if the Arsalian army is here then the Feorian must be nearby.

The girls' hopes dwindle however when they stop seeing what they believe are the Arsalian armies' fire lights but are not met with Feoria's.

Alice asks in frustration questions she had many times the last few nights, "Where are they?

Are we in Feoria yet?"

"I don't know, keep lookin'. They gotta be down there somewhere," Danahlia calls from behind the Tokala.

"It is possible," Twinkaleni shouts over the swiftly passing night air, "That the Feorian army has been routed or even retreated to more secure positions in preparation for the coming winter."

"But the scouts were lookin' for a way through the Vipuado," says Alice.

"They were days away by flight, weeks by foot. They may not be aware of current movements," Twinkaleni answers, peering down around Squiggles' thick neck.

"Guys, look!" Danahlia calls, pointing around Alice. Following her finger, Alice notes a darkness deeper than the night stabbing at the sky. "A mountain," calls Danahlia, "We should set down there, figure out what to do." Agreeing, Alice guides Squiggles toward it.

"Do you recognize it?" asks Twinkaleni.

"Nope, but we've come far enough to deserve a rest. That Order of yours might have magic, but they can't fly. It'll be a good while before they can-" a piercing short screech interrupts Danahlia.

"The tick was that?" Alice asks in alarm, fox ears angling around for the sound. In all the times they had flown atop Squiggles they had never heard anything of the sort before. They had a hard enough time just hearing each other over the dragon's wing beats and the rushing air.

They hear it again, but now it's joined by others.

Twinkaleni squeaks, "Look!" pointing below and off to the left. Rising from the dark landscape come huge flapping forms.

At first, Alice thinks their some strange birds, but watching their silhouettes steadily become more defined as they close in she starts to identify various features she vaguely recognizes. Large ears extending to either side of blunt wide faces, wings with crescents of stretched skin coming to points similar to Squiggles' own, and short featherless tails, tell Alice they're, "Bats!" she calls to the others. Though these weren't the minuscule flying rodents occasionally seen at dusk back home. Each of the winged beasts is easily several times larger than herself, still greatly dwarfed by Squiggles, but their numbers seem to give them the confidence to challenge even him. A dozen or more of the dark shapes are heading directly toward them.

"Ticks! What do you think they want?!" Danahlia shouts over the bat swarm's piercing cries.

Twinkaleni, observing the flying beasts, calls, "They can't possibly mean us harm, they're far too small to face Squiggles!" Squiggles seems to agree and ignores them for the most part, until they get closer.

The girls look on nervously as the bats take positions around Squiggles as if investigating the dragon, their piercing shrieks loud. Alice feels Danahlia shifting behind her and sees the Liguna trying to pull the bow free from their things. Squiggles doesn't care for the noisy company and erupts with a deafening roar, the girls feeling his neck vibrate under them. The bats immediately scatter in a wild panic, and for a moment the girls think they're safe, but the bats begin to gather once more around them.

Alice spots one getting close, just over and to the right of them. She notices a strange lump on it's back, smooth not fuzzy like the rest of the giant bat's outline. As the bat maneuvers closer, in between rapid flaps of it's wings, the lump moves, revealing itself to be a slim, Cold Blood man.

As Alice calls, "They've riders!" to her friends, the man shifts sharply and an arrow shatters against the hard scales of Squiggles' neck, sending splinters over Alice's legs.

"They're attacking!" cries Twinkaleni.

Danahlia shouts something in Feorian that gives the man pause, but then Alice sees him nock another arrow, and more missiles begin zipping past them. Squiggles roars angrily and drifts toward the nearest of the bats, forcing it to back away or be knocked from the air by a beating wing. Danahlia continues shouting to the bat riders, but they seem intent on bringing the dragon down. One makes the mistake of flying ahead of Squiggles and tries to fire back at the girls. The dragon bathes the bat in fire, sweeping his fiery breath over of few others. Alice watches in horror as the bats and their riders plummet in flames, screaming to the earth.

"Squigs, no!" Danahlia cries.

"They are attacking, we *must* defend ourselves!" shouts Twinkaleni. She then extends a hand to a rider trying to fire on them from above, calling, "Vespis Flomino!"

An invisible force smashes into the bat, sending it and it's rider flailing away. Alice watches as the bat manages to regain itself and immediately dives after it's rider. Squiggles roars in pain and Alice sees an arrow lodged in his neck, having managed to pass between his thick scales. She can feel the dragon preparing to shift and grabs Twinkaleni around the waist with one hand, gripping a strap with the other, while calling to her companions, "Hold on!"

Squiggles swiftly spins around to face the swarm of foes, flapping his wings and roaring his outrage. Alice holds tight to the angry dragon's neck with her legs as she and her friends are swung about. The move surprises the bats and one is clipped by a wing, sending it's rider sailing into the night as the others spread out and keep firing. Squiggles goes on the offensive and snaps with his jaws at the nearest bat, missing but then launching a wide, sweeping cone of flame at it and the others. Several are hit and sent burning to the ground as still more continue their assault. The girls can only desperately press them selves against the enraged reptile's neck and hold on.

Alice closes her eyes, leaning hard over Twinkaleni as she holds the Murin and the reigns, feeling Danahlia do the same behind her. She hears the riders screaming and their bats screeching. She feels the dragon swinging about, the vibration in his throat, and the heat of his flame. After a short but harrowing battle, the sky quiets and Alice opens her eyes. What is left of the bats and their riders flee for the black forest below. Squiggles bleeds from many wounds but flies proudly on, roaring after his retreating foes.

Breathing hard, Alice calls, "Is anybody hurt?"

Twinkaleni shakes her head and Alice turns the best she can, "Danny?"

The Liguna looks off at nothing, her eyes wide in horror. Alice nudges her with her shoulder getting the lizard girl's attention, "Danny? Are you ok?" Danahlia gives a brief nod without looking back at her.

Twinkaleni pulls another arrow free that had managed to stick between the dragon's scales, "We should assess Squiggles' wounds."

Alice agrees, rubbing the dragon's neck while giving him the command to descend. She directs Squiggles to land near the peak of the forest covered mountain. Some fortune finds them as a small glittering spring resides in the clearing they choose. Squiggles lands heavily and immediately makes his way to the water. Alice and Twinkaleni slide down the dragon as he drinks but Danahlia stays put.

Worried, Alice looks up to her, "Danny? Are you hurt?"

Danahlia looks down at her, eyes unblinking, "We killed 'em. We killed 'em, Alice."

Alice frowns deeply but Twinkaleni, looking

under Squiggles for anymore arrows, says, "We had little choice. They attacked us. And to be perfectly fair, Squiggles killed them." The dragon rumbles at his name while he drinks.

Danahlia looks sharply at the Murin. "They were defendin' their lands! Probably thought we were tryin' to sneak in and attack 'em! And Squigs wouldn't be here if we didn't bring 'em. We did it, we all did!" she insists, then more to herself, "I murdered my own people."

"Danny," Alice tries consolingly, "It couldn't be helped. It was a misunderstanding."

Danahlia says nothing, only looking down at her hands. Alice decides to join Twinkaleni in checking Squiggles' wounds. He has a handful of arrows in him, but thanks to his thick hide, none manage to pierce deeply. He doesn't even seem to mind when the girls pull them out, more interested in drinking and resting. There are a few other larger wounds, perhaps bites or claw marks left by the bats, and his wings have a few holes in them, but otherwise the dragon simply seems tired. After he drinks, he curls up and lays down, letting the girls do what they can to clean his injuries.

Danahlia slides off the dragon and leans against him looking more dower than Alice had ever seen her. Alice considers her words and then tries, "They were really brave warriors." Danahlia looks up at this so she continues, "To protect their lands and people by facing a dragon, the first to do it in like a thousand years."

"More like two hundred," corrects Twinkaleni.

"Still, I'm sure they'll be remembered. They'll have songs sung about their courage and sacrifice," says Alice.

"Yeah, maybe," Danahlia replies solemnly.

Hungry but too worn out to worry about it, the girls join Squiggles in a nap.

A short time later, Alice is jolted awake by an angry male cry in Feorian. Squiggles growls, shifting to rise, causing Alice to slide off his leg and into the grass. She sits up, alert but bleary eyed.

She sees Danahlia standing next to her saying something and pointing but her words are drowned out by the war cries of the dozens of armed and armored Cold Bloods charging at them in the dim morning sun. This in turn is drowned out by Squiggles, roaring his challenge just over her. The sound is so loud, the air feels like it's shaking and Alice has trouble maintaining her balance even sitting. Squiggles opens his wings threateningly to the oncoming Cold Bloods as Danahlia races ahead of him to place herself between the Feorians and the dragon.

The Liguna waves her arms frantically and seems to be shouting to her people but all Alice can hear is a high pitched whine she can't shake from her ears. She isn't sure if it's Danahlia's words or the dragon's fury but many of the Cold Blood warriors slow, some even stopping. As Danahlia continues to wave wildly, most of the Feorians give pause and look to each other in confusion. The only one that doesn't stop is a particularly large male. Alice had never seen his species before. The heavily scarred man stands nearly as large as an Urock but with a long muzzle filled with teeth that reminds her of the sawtooths the girls had encountered along the Great Horn's water ways. He is easily three times the girth of Danahlia, who stands unmoving perhaps only ten yards away, but the massive man notices the other warriors have stopped following and turns to them angrily. He wears thick looking leather armor studded with short spikes that, as far as Alice could tell, may very will be part of his rough looking skin. More alarming are the many skulls he has dangling from ropes hanging over his shoulders to wrap around his waste. They are large, mostly white but some pink, and despite not knowing for sure, Alice feels strangely certain they're all from Warm Bloods. When he turns, Alice can see a large, wide cleaver of some sort hanging on his back, and from all the stains, it looks well used.

As the massive man yells to the other warriors, Twinkaleni and Alice nervously arm themselves, though with so many of the Cold Bloods wielding bows, Alice isn't sure how much good it will do. Worse, while the man shouts and points, more Feorians appear, pushing up from the rear to see what's going on. Alice's hearing slowly returns to her and she can just make out Danahlia and the man's shouting over the murmur of the now hundred or so Cold Blood warriors. Squiggles is getting restless but Alice tries to keep him calm, hoping Danahlia might get them out of this without the need for a fight.

Danahlia addresses her people and states her name, though the rest of what she says is in some Feorian tongue. The frighteningly large man says something back, pointing toward Alice, Twinkaleni, and Squiggles. After several more exchanges, the man glares at Danahlia and raises a hand high, bellowing something that sounds like, "Ahjani!"

The other warriors pass the word around and slowly begin to chant, with voices steadily growing in number, "Ah ja ni! Ah ja ni! Ah ja ni!"

Danahlia glares back at the man then looks out at her people who continue chanting. Alice begins to shake uncontrollably, not knowing what is about to happen but not liking any of it. Squiggles stamps his feet and flaps his wings in agitation but stays put, Alice keeping before him. Eventually, Danahlia raises her hand high, just like the man, and they both close them into fists. A few of the Feorians cheer but most continue chanting, though more quietly. With that, the dwarfed Liguna girl returns to her companions.

"What is happening?" demands Twinkaleni, a small knife in her hand.

Frowning deeply, Danahlia says, "Well, they

saw us battle the bat riders and then land up here. The big guy says we're sneakin' into Feoria to burn their villages and cities while all the warriors are away. I said we're not. He says I'm a traitor and helping you furries. I said I'm an Ashclaw returning home. He says I'm a liar. I said he's full of... stuff, and now he wants to, uh, duel to see whose right."

"Duel? That guy?" Alice asks looking at the imposing man, his muscular arms crossed over his wide chest, waiting impatiently. "That's crazy, that, that's not even fair."

"I know, he needs at *least* three more guys backin' 'im up," Danahlia smirks, removing her spear from their things.

"No, Danny, you can't," Alice pleads, "He'll kill you!"

"Gee, thanks. I don't know what I'm gonna do with all this confidence you're loadin' me up with," tosses back Danahlia, stretching her arms.

"I will duel him in your stead," announces Twinkaleni, "His size will be of little use against my-"

"No!" commands Danahlia, "This is between two warriors. It can't be settled any other way."

"Then let's go. We can just fly away, find somewhere else, far from here. An island or something," begs Alice, grabbing her love's arm.

Danahlia looks into Alice's eyes for a moment but doesn't let herself get trapped there, "No. This is important. This isn't just about me. If I run, I won't ever be allowed back. The Ashclaw name won't mean anything anymore. I can't do that to my family." Danahlia runs a hand over Alice's ears and down the back of her neck, "No worries. I can take him."

Alice clings to the Liguna's arm, tears in her eyes, "No, Danny, no."

Danahlia pulls herself free and begins making her way back to the massive man, "It's the way it's gotta be. You two should get on Squigs. If I go down, you're not gonna wanna be here."

"Please, let's just go!" Alice begs, trying to follow but Twinkaleni tugs on her pant leg.

"Do not fear," Twinkaleni says up to her, "Danny will not fall."

Alice can only look on and try to keep Squiggles calm as Danahlia spins her spear about her in an elegant dance. The large man isn't impressed, though the other Cold Bloods cheer and spread to watch while keeping well away from Squiggles. Danahlia's spinning brings her a few feet away from the much larger Cold Blood. She suddenly stops, holding her spear before her in two hands, point extended. The man doesn't budge, arms still crossed, standing with all the confidence of a mountain being met by a breeze. Danahlia steps forward with a lightning quick lunge aimed right for the man's face, but he anticipates it and ducks, spinning to bring around his long, thick tail. The heavy looking appendage slams into Danahlia's legs before she can recover from her strike and knocks her to the ground.

"Danny!" Alice can't help but screech as the Liguna immediately rolls away, keeping her spear extended to the man. The man doesn't bother giving chase, only turns back toward his opponent, slab like arms still crossed, a grin along his toothy muzzle. As Danahlia gets to her feet, the man pulls his absurdly large cleaver like weapon from his back. Danahlia begins a swift series of thrusts targeted at random areas of the man's body. The man's cleaver is so wide he can hold it before him like a shield and blocks much of the attack. The man steps into Danahlia's assault, attempting to take away her range advantage. A thrust glances off the man's leg as he steps forward but it does little to deter him. Danahlia continues her attack, stepping back, tail sweeping behind her to make sure the path is clear. She aims her thrusts high and low, forcing the man to block or endure more small wounds.

The man crouches, getting more of himself behind his cleaver as he advances, reducing the available target area for Danahlia. The Liguna tries to circle around to his side, but the man lashes out with his thick tail, forcing Danahlia to remain before him. Off balance, Danahlia makes a hard thrust at the man's fingers to drive him back and regain her footing. This seemed to be what the man had been waiting for. He crouches lower and surges forth the moment she strikes the broad side of his weapon, knocking her to her back. With surprising speed, the man rushes over her and raises his great cleaver above his head, intent on splitting the Liguna in two.

Alice, trying to keep an increasingly agitated Squiggles calm, hears Twinkaleni murmur beside her, "Gravitus."

The moment the man, already roaring his triumph, attempts to bring his weapon crashing down atop Danahlia's prone body, it slips from his hands and clatters heavily to the ground behind him. Before he even knows what happened Danahlia takes advantage, sweeping her spear at his legs. She scores a cut along his shins and the man growls more in anger than pain. He swings his tail hard at Danahlia, but she's already rolling away and avoids it. The man takes up his blade once more, testing it's heft before turning back to his opponent.

No longer interested in defense, the man charges wildly at Danahlia, again with speed belying the man's size, his cleaver held back to make a wide horizontal slash. The lizard girl only just manages to dive to the side to avoid the attack, but the man uses his own momentum to spin, immediately turning to follow her, this time attempting a diagonal cut. Danahlia manages to dive out of the way again, just as Twinkaleni murmurs, "Gravitus," once more. The man's weapon slams into the earth, burying itself to the handle. The moment Danahlia regains some balance, she thrusts at the man's right thigh, scoring a hit that makes the man roar in rage. Forgetting his cleaver, he turns on Danahlia and charges at her with his bare clawed hands.

Danahlia keeps her spear before her but the man shifts, letting the point slip under one bulky bicep. One of the bracing arms of her boar spear catches under the man's arm pit as his claws reach toward Danahlia's face. The Liguna steps aside, bracing her spear against the man's arm and letting his momentum carry him past her while giving him a cut under the caught arm. Not deterred in the least, the man swings for her with his other hand. Danahlia has to step away, abandoning her spear to avoid the blow only for the man to spin, slamming his tail into her chest. She's hit hard and sent flying back a few feet before tumbling gracelessly to the ground.

The man looks at the new wound under his arm in disgust, letting the pain fuel his anger further. With a vicious roar, he charges at the downed girl again, fists raised like hammers. Squiggles begins moving toward the fighting pair, but Alice keeps herself before him. She's about to call Twinkaleni for help and sees the mage make a slight gesture, murmuring, "Telefuss."

Only a yard from Danahlia, one of the man's clawed, pounding feet suddenly slams into his other, sending the man crashing to the ground face first. Before he can recover, Danahlia leaps atop his back, holding a bone bladed knife to his throat shouting what Alice figures is some command to yield.

The fight has taken the combatants more toward the Cold Bloods, so she can't hear the man's reply, but the Cold Blood warriors, having become silent, now cheer loudly for the victor. Danahlia stands over the fallen man, knife held high in one fist. Alice cheers too, dashing over to her love. After a moment to absorb her triumph, Danahlia drops her knife and turns to walk toward Alice, filthy and exhausted but smiling. The crowd of Cold Bloods cheer different words but Alice feels she can definitely make out some of them calling, "Ashclaw, Ashclaw, Ashclaw!"

Alice crashes into Danahlia, wrapping her arms around her and gripping tight. Danahlia cries out, "Ah! Easy, easy!" Alice jerks away, apologizing, and the Liguna lifts her shirt to reveal a large, wide bruise over much of her stomach.

Alice falls to her knees upon seeing it, her hands immediately reaching to feel around the discolored skin, "Oh ticks, are you ok?"

Danahlia winces, "Yeah, just, a little tender."

Twinkaleni comes to join them with a satisfied grin, "Well fought. Your people certainly seem to approve. This should aid us greatly in, LOOK OUT!"

The Murin points. Alice peers around Danahlia's hip to the massive man charging at a full tilt, mad rage in his eyes. He's on them in a second, large open jaws tilted to the side as he bites at Danahlia's head. Just before his jaws can snap shut, Squiggles' far larger set closes around the man's torso from above and behind. The dragon picks the man up with ease, his legs kicking, just before giving him a little toss, much like a bird with a freshly caught fish. The Cold Blood warriors cry out in alarm as Squiggles crunches wetly on one of their largest, blood dripping to the earth.

The warriors raise their weapons and take aim with bows as Squiggles swallows and then opens his wings threateningly to them. Danahlia puts herself between them once more, speaking to them as Alice and Twinkaleni try to keep the dragon from doing any more. Eventually, Squiggles lowers his wings and the Feorians lower their weapons. After a time talking among themselves with Danahlia, a few of the warriors, four men and one woman, leave their arms and approach with the Liguna. Perhaps to show their courage or simply too in awe over seeing a creature thought to be extinct, the handful of Cold Bloods make their way toward Alice, Twinkaleni, and Squiggles.

Proud, powerful, and confident the Cold Bloods could do him little harm even if they tried, Squiggles does not feel the need to threaten any further. He does, however, keep a watchful eye on the warriors even as Alice assures him they are safe. Tentatively, some of the handful come forth and are allowed to place their hands on Squiggles' thick hind legs and tail. Seeing this, many of the other warriors are suddenly eager to step forth, but Squiggles gives a throaty rumble, showing his disinterest in so many approaching at once. The few that got to touch him retreat back into their ranks and are quickly surrounded as they talk excitedly of their experience. Danahlia says these are the war party's leaders. The large man Squiggles ate was one too, though by attacking Danahlia's back after their duel he had lost all status according to the others.

After further discussion, the leaders return to Danahlia to announce that she has proven in the eyes of all present that she is who she claims to be and that they would like to be the first to welcome the long lost Ashclaw home. The Cold Bloods cheer her return and Danahlia revels in it. Eventually, the war party's leaders gather their warriors and have them begin the march back down to their camp. Two remain, a fit but not terribly imposing Molocie man and the female. Alice isn't sure what species she is, but she resembles a Liguna though with a shorter muzzle and large bulbous eyes more akin to a frog. The pair reveal they are as fluent in Arsalian as Danahlia and are eager to hear her tale. Danahlia, never shy about telling stories, shares it as they make their way down the mountain.

They speak in Arsalian, letting Alice and Twinkaleni listen, answer questions, and add their own commentary. They tell them that their war party is only a small part of a larger warband currently harassing the Arsalians further east. Their small detachment is charged with keeping and fortifying the mountain, the warband's fall back point for the coming winter. Alice asks about the possibility that her father might be imprisoned somewhere in Feoria. The frog featured woman, who Danahlia says is a Pakua, tells them that it is possible but they themselves have no such prisoner. She also says that Danahlia's uncle, Javas Ashclaw, leads a much larger warband to the southwest and will likely know more. Excited by the news, the girls decide to stay and rest with the Pakua, Simonia's party, making plans to depart the next morning for Danahlia's uncle.

The Cold Blood's mountain camp doesn't look like much, a few fire pits and temporary dwellings, until it's revealed that the vast majority of the base is not on, but inside the mountain itself. The area's natural caves were claimed and greatly expanded by the Cold Bloods digging an intricate system of tunnels that emerge over much of the mountain's eastern slope. Favoring tactics that allowed them to hit hard and disappear before the enemy could mount an effective counter, the tunnels dug would allow Feorian warriors to strike an incoming enemy from any direction and then vanish below the earth only to reappear elsewhere. The network still needed work and so the majority of the force stationed on the mountain were sent to distract the

Warm Blood armies so the tunnelers could labor in relative peace.

The two leaders are proud of their work and show the girls to one of the tunnel network's entrances. It's small and cleverly made to appear as just a part of it's rocky outcropping. This makes it difficult to see unless you're right on top of it and prevents enemies from assaulting in numbers. This also means Squiggles can't get in, so the girls decide to stay on the surface. The leaders struggle to get their people back to work on their tunnels, the Feorian's too distracted by the dragon among them. None had ever seen one and only know of them through old stories. Eventually, the leaders decide to give the tunnelers the day off to morn their fallen comrades and celebrate Danahlia's return to them.

Food in the form of massive grub like worms are brought up from the tunnels and placed over the fires. Found in the mountain and now bred for food, the girls are told the worms make up a large portion of the Feorian's diet here. These are served with various roots and potato like tubers made into stews, mashed, or simply boiled till soft. Alice finds the worms to be rather appetizing, chewy and tasting of nutty mushrooms. Squiggles is given some whole and eats them glutinously. He also finds the dump pile for rocks brought up from the tunnels and dines on these as well. Many Feorians are greatly fascinated by the dragon and seem to truly enjoy watching him munch on stones.

The leaders ask questions about him, wanting to know where he was found, if there are more in Arsalia, how old he is, his diet, his fire, and many other things. The girls answer truthfully, mostly because Danahlia blurts answers without a hint of guile. The leaders seem particularly relieved to hear he is the only one they are aware of. Before they had disappeared from the known world, dragons were considered the greatest of weapons, giving their masters tremendous power while forcing their enemies to kneel or burn.

At night, the girls sleep atop Squiggles as they generally did when away from shelter. The dragon sleeps curled on his side and lets the girls use one of his wings as a blanket, his body heat keeping them warm against the cooling fall air. Simonia has guards posted to watch over them. She says it is just in case the man Squiggles ate's clansmen try to take some form of vengeance. The girls, however, wake peacefully the next morning and prepare for the next portion of their journey.

Simonia has decided that she will lead the girls herself to Danahlia's Uncle's camp. She takes them to what appears to be an abyss in the side of the mountain. It looks to be a natural, stone mouthed hole in the ground, large enough that even Squiggles could easily enter, and seems to go straight down into empty darkness. Alice doesn't get close enough to look far into it but she can hear the familiar screech of bats. Simonia says this is were they keep their flying mounts, who generally like to sleep during the day. The trust between the Pakua woman and her bat are so great that she simply calls to it before letting herself fall into the blackness. Seconds later, she emerges atop a large, dark gray colored bat. It screeches in alarm upon seeing Squiggles and the dragon rumbles back, but both are kept calm with soothing words and pets. Once the mounts adjust to one another, the girls board Squiggles and take to the air, following Simonia and her great bat southward.

Chapter 10

The Red

The trip takes several days even flying. During the trek, Squiggles and Simonia's bat, Barak, both proud creatures, seem to race each other, Squiggles flying with more energy than usual while Simonia admits her bat is doing the same. When they land to rest, Barak prefers to cling to the thick trunks of large trees, using sharp thumb like extensions protruding from his wings to dig into the shaded wood under wide branches. Simonia's harness is made so she can remain comfortably attached to her bat even while he rests in this manner.

The Pakua woman knows this land well. As such, she can pick spots that have clean water and are relatively danger free. Once, they stay in what used to be a village, now only a ruin but at least with a functional well. Simonia tells the girls that this is a common sight so close to the border between Arsalia and Feoria. The many smaller territories along the borders where frequently a place of contention but still managed to prosper due largely to trade. Once the war began, armies from both sides would march across fields, devour crops, burn homes, cut down forests, and hunt the life from the land. Now, the border territories that were once fought over are mostly barren, void of all but a few hardy weeds sandwiched between too hate driven forces. Forces only fueled to cross to the other side by the death inflicted the last time one dared do so.

They follow an impressive river, the Elois, that acts as a natural border between the two prime nations. On either bank, Alice begins to notice people looking up at them. They stick to the western side and she can easily tell those below are Cold Bloods, while just making out that the eastern shore is lined with Warm Bloods, the mountainous, rounded shapes of Urocks standing out among the other varied soldiers. With Simonia leading with her bat and well out of range of the eastern bank, they fly assured they will not come under attack. For miles the groups along the river steadily become larger, their camps stretching well away from the river until there are hundreds looking and pointing at them from the ground.

The Warm and Cold blood warriors tend to be thickest at narrower points of the Elois and

Twinkaleni suggests they are meant to guard against possible crossing. The river becomes particularly narrow at a point and it is clear that the bulk of both Arsalia and Feoria's armies are here. Stretching far back from the river are camps filled with what might be thousands of people. From the look of all the fortified structures, Alice guesses they have been here for some time. It's difficult for her to believe that after so many years of war, the nations still have such numbers to devote to fighting. Simonia leads her bat off to the west and begins to descend, so Alice has Squiggles do the same.

The Pakua woman lands in a large open area made by clearing the surrounding forest's tall trees. A great many people are drawn to the site as Squiggles slowly descends as well. A few immediately come to greet Simonia, though everyone keeps their distance from Squiggles, who doesn't seem to like all the attention. He swings his head about to keep watch over the gathering crowd while making disagreeable grumbles. The girls dismount and move to calm him, knowing he will feel better once he is fed and given water.

Upon dismounting, Simonia's bat flies off to some nearby trees, hanging upon them as he likes to in the shade among more of his kind. After some discussion, Simonia and those speaking with her make their way to Alice, Twinkaleni, and Danahlia, cradling and petting Squiggles' massive head.

The dragon rumbles at their approach giving them pause, though the girls assure them they will not be harmed. Still, they hesitate and Danahlia goes forth to meet with them. They seem very pleased to see her and wave her to a squat wide structure made of stone and wood. Before they can take a step, a Liguna man bursts from the building's open door. He looks very much like Danahlia save for being taller and having darker brown skin. Another man, also a Liguna but lime green in color points Danahlia out to him.

The moment the darker of them spots her, he unceremoniously dashes to her calling, "Danahlia!"

Danahlia calls back, "Zhisha!" and races to meet him.

The too embrace, their tails intertwining as they do. Alice and Twinkaleni watch the touching reunion, seeing Danahlia's uncle brought to tears as he tells his niece something in Feorian.

Two large men of the same or similar species to the sawtooth like man Squiggles had eaten have also emerged from the building to flank Danahlia's uncle. They are armored in plate and leather, each wielding heavy looking spears. Alice figures they must be Danahlia's Uncle's body guards. Both look distastefully to Squiggles, no doubt wondering how they would defend their charge from such a creature. Squiggles glares back at them but does little else.

Danahlia brings her uncle to meet her friends, when she does, the large bodyguards follow. Getting too close for Squiggles' taste, the dragon rasps at them. Danahlia says nonchalant that Squiggles doesn't like Crocorosie and her uncle simply holds up a hand, making the imposing men stop in their tracks. Danahlia happily announces, "This is Alice and Twinkie. Their the reason I survived over there."

The Murin mage immediately steps forward, bowing, "Twinka-"

Alice is about to introduce herself as well, but Danahlia's uncle crouches to lift up Twinkaleni in one arm and wraps the other around Alice before she can say a word, pulling them in to a hard hug saying quietly from between them in accented but perfectly understandable Arsalian, "Brought back my blood to me you did. Dhis debt. I will repay it."

Before the girls can even reply, the man is pushed roughly back, Squiggles shoving his own enormous head in where Danahlia's uncle's just was. "And this is Squiggles. He's a dragon," says Danahlia, gesturing to him.

To Alice's surprise, the man does not back down from Squiggles' glare despite the fact that the dragon could easily fit him in his mouth whole. In fact, the Liguna man meets the massive reptile's stare with his own. The now substantial gathering of warriors goes silent around them and Alice becomes worried, not knowing what Squiggles might do. He wasn't used to strangers not immediately showing some level of fear around him. But after a few tense seconds, Squiggles just snorts in the man's face, hard enough to make the Liguna draw back, before turning his attention to the hundreds around them.

Everyone but Danahlia's uncle seems to let out a sigh of relief, the Liguna man only wiping his face with a wide grin to his niece, "You made very interesting friends." Then to the other girls he says, "You must be hungry after such a long journey." He half turns to the green Liguna that had accompanied him, "Prepare a feast and gather the (he says a word Alice doesn't understand)" Then in a louder voice he announces, "Now, we celebrate the return of our long lost daughtah!"

The gathered warriors cheer enthusiastically.

In the clearing, many large clay pots containing water are dumped into a trough carved from the trunk of a great tree. This, along with various dried meats, are offered to Squiggles, possibly in the hopes that he will not wander too far and into the animal pens Alice had seen dotting the vast camp. Once he is satisfied, the girls are taken to be washed and clothed, their own clothes, never fancy, having become worn and tattered. The girls have little time to enjoy their bath as they are rushed to clean and dress by a few female attendants. By the time they are deemed presentable enough, a great gathering has taken place in Danahlia's uncle, Javas', command building.

They are told that the leaders of the many warriors, some thousands, making up Javas' massive warband have joined him and now await to be introduced to the girls. Hearing this makes Alice distinctly uncomfortable but she has little time to dwell on it, for they are quickly taken to stand before Javas and those that serve under him.

The command building looked plenty wide from the outside, but with so many squeezing within it now, it feels terribly cramped. The girls are led through a crowd that looks at them with many strange eyes. The diversity of the Cold Bloods gathered astonishes Alice and she can't help but stare about, open mouthed, as she is guided and lightly pushed onward. Twinkaleni seems even more uncomfortable than she, being considerably smaller than everyone and having to look up much of the time. Danahlia strides on ahead, confident as usual, almost marching while she beams at the attention.

When they come to a stop a few feet before Javas, standing before a decorated chair and flanked by his guards, he announces with open arms, "We great chiefs gather now, not to talk war but to celebrate the return of one of our daughtahs!" He speaks in Arsalian, which Alice sees many seem to understand, though some have translators, as they all rumble with approval. "Thought lost to us,

Danahlia of clan Ashclaw has survived in the Warm Blood lands since the war began!" The room's rumbles grow as Danahlia joins her uncle and he has to shout over them, "She is proof that our modahs and fadahs, our brodahs and sistahs, our soons and our daughtahs, not seen since calmer times, may yet return to us!"

The building shakes with cheers, becoming so loud Alice has to press her ears against her head and sees Twinkaleni do the same, though it's difficult not to feel their joy. After several minutes of thunderous cheers, croaks, hoots, hollers, and other noises Alice has no words for, Javas manages to bring back silence so he can continue, "I, Javas Ashclaw, Warchief of clan Ashclaw and dhis mighty warband, am grateful to know that she did not need to survive alone. At great dangah to demselves, friends of Danahlia and now friends of clan Ashclaw, Alice and Twinkie have journeyed here togedah, where day are most welcome guests under my roof."

The gathering says the girls names aloud to the best of their ability and Twinkaleni sighs. The girls are then pushed forward and walk to stand beside Danahlia, but then are moved by the attendants to stand before Javas while the gathered leaders practice and discuss how best to say their names.

Danahlia's uncle smiles warmly at the two girls before him. The moment he speaks all go silent once more, "Alice and Twinkie. You have braved many dangahs to bring my blood back to me. For dhis, I am in your debt. If there is anything you would ask of me, speak it, and if it is in my powah, it will be yours."

Alice looks nervously to Twinkaleni who urges her on. Alice knows what she has to do but feeling the expectant eyes of so many strangers on her makes it difficult to think. Alice looks nervously from the great man before her, the two massive men behind him, and then to Danahlia, who smiles and nods encouragingly.

Alice swallows and in a quavering voice starts, "I heard that, maybe, you had my dad." Or at least that's what she thinks she said though Javas' eyes widen a bit, clearly not understanding. She tries again. "I heard that sometimes you take prisoners, after a fight, and my dad, they said he was, dead, but then I heard you, take prisoners, and that he might be one so we came to see if, he was still alive," she stammers, feeling terribly inadequate to be standing before all these people.

Javas places a hand on her shoulder, steadying the quavering girl, saying simply, "Name him."

Alice, nearly coming to tears, looks at the man, "R-robert, Robert Dippleblack."

Javas looks up and off to the side in thought, asking seemingly to himself, "Why I know dhis name?" The green Liguna from before leans in from where he had been standing, near completely obscured by Danahlia, and whispers something to him. Danahlia's uncle's eyes widen again, "Robert dah Red?" He then looks to Alice very seriously, "Robert dah Red is your fadah?"

Alice had never heard this name before. Immediately she is struck with an overwhelming dread, sure that it had all been some mistake, that her father had been dead all these years and she had come all this way, done so much, dared to hope, had the audacity to dream, all for nothing.

Then Javas grins, "Yes, I can see him in you. Your eyes. Strong like his." He then puts up fingers beside his head, "Got his eahs too."

Alice suddenly feels out of breath but still tries to say, "If, you have him, can you, please, let him go?"

She isn't entirely sure what she actually said but Javas places both steadying hands on Alice's shoulders while giving the green Liguna a half turn saying, "Have him brought, go."

The green Liguna seems to protest, whispering something in Danahlia's Uncle's ear that he clearly doesn't like. Javas glares at the man, "I gave my word. Bring him now." With that, the man is dismissed and Javas turns his attention back to the shaky fox girl, grinning widely while shaking his head in disbelief, "You are Robert dah Red's daughtah?"

Still uncertain, Alice says in a quiet voice, "I don't know. My dad's name is Robert Dippleblack."

Still smiling Javas tells her, "Ah yes, dah Red. Dhis name we gave him. He, very skilled with sword. Aftah a battle, we heah his fur is coated red with the blood of our warriahs. I have him, Alice Dippleblack, and if you wish him free, this is what I will do." He then nods after his green skinned attendant saying quietly just for Alice, "He thinks me crazy for letting Robert dah Red go, and maybe I am, but *I* am warchief. That mean he has to do what I say."

Alice lets out a breath still not wanting to let herself believe this could be happening, that she might actually be getting her father back after all this time. Danahlia grabs her up in her arms and squeezes her hard, keeping Alice from toppling over. She's saying something but Alice can't hear it over her own thoughts.

After a few moments to let it sink in, Javas gives his head a little shake, smiling, "One fights us in a war and another comes among thousands of us to get him back. Dah Dippleblacks are a brave bunch."

Part of Alice wants to leap for joy, while another wants to burst into tears, and a third just wants to lay down. Various other feelings storm through her until they smash into a wall when she hears what Twinkaleni asks of Danahlia's uncle.

The Murin says plainly, "I would be most grateful for an escort back to the northern border. I would like to return to Arsalia as soon as possible."

Javas is nearly as surprised as Alice and Danahlia.

Danahlia looks down at the tiny mage, "Twinkie?"

"But why?" Alice asks.

Twinkaleni only looks to Javas, "Is this possible?"

Javas nods slowly, "It can be done, of course, but at least enjoy the celebration. Let me show you my gratitude for all that you have done for my family. As long as I am chief, you will be most welcome heah."

Twinkaleni lowers her gaze and shakes her head, "I assure you, if I could leave immediately that would be more than adequate."

Javas raises a brow to Danahlia and then looks to one of his guards, giving the large man a quick nod. The guard steps forward to lead Twinkaleni away, but before she can take a step Danahlia grabs her as Alice crouches down beside her.

"Twinkie, what gives? We just got here. I think we earned a little down time," reasons Danahlia.

"We can't go now, they're bringin' my dad, he's here, he might really be here," insists Alice.

"Not we. You two will stay here. I will go alone," replies Twinkaleni shortly.

Danahlia's brow furrows, "What are you talkin' about? We're not gonna let you go alone, you know that."

"Yeah," agrees Alice, "Just wait a little bit. We can get my dad and take Squiggles wherever you want."

The small mouse girl pulls away from Danahlia, surprising her long time companions by shouting, "No!" She calms herself before continuing, "The two of you will be much safer here. Danahlia, you are finally among your people, you should not leave them. And Alice, you may be reunited with your father. Under the protection of Danahlia's uncle, you can live out the rest of the war here in Feoria. I must return to Arsalia to free my own people. I cannot afford to wait."

The taller girls press but Twinkaleni returns hotly, "I thank you for journeying with me this far, but this is not your fight. I will not have you risk yourselves for purposes that are solely my own."

The girls press again for the Murin to reconsider but then she shouts more furiously, "NO! I will not be burdened by your foolishness any longer! If you dare try to follow me..." the air becomes strangely constricting and everyone gathered makes sounds of surprise as Twinkaleni's eyes change from amber to glow gold, "I will force you back here myself!"

Shocked into silence, the girls only watch as their friend storms off, though Alice feels sure she saw a tear just before Twinkaleni turned from them. The Murin gives the guard charged with escorting her a quick look and he immediately gets back to his duty, leading her out of the building, the alarmed crowd yielding swiftly before them.

Javas says to Danahlia, "Interesting friends indeed."

Growing murmuring over what just transpired snaps Alice back and she rises, telling Danahlia, "We have to go after her."

Danahlia stays put, saying solemnly, "You heard what she said. She doesn't want us to."

Alice turns to Danahlia, surprised, "No, we have to-"

"She's right," Danahlia interrupts, "We've been holdin' her back."

Alice's brow furrows, "What?"

"We kept trying to keep her from using her magic, getting stronger like she wants to. Maybe if she figures it out, you know, really cuts loose she can free the mages from that Order."

Alice shakes her head, tears welling in her eyes, "No. What if she gets killed? She's so small and-"

"And she's more powerful than both of us put together," Danahlia finishes, "We can't stop 'er."

Alice feels anger welling inside of her, anger that Danahlia would give up, and anger that she's right. The fox girl races out of the building only to find a massive crowd of unfamiliar Cold Bloods before her and no sign of Twinkaleni.

She calls out to the Feorians, "Did you see her? Which way did she go?" The Cold Bloods only look at her in incomprehension. Alice frantically signs with her hands Twinkaleni's large round ears and glowing eyes, but the crowd only murmurs to each other in confusion. Alice begins trying to push her way through them, but they're so thick she quickly looses hope. Sagging in defeat, she eventually manages to find her way back to the command building some time later. It's empty now save for Danahlia in tears being comforted by her uncle. She joins her love in sharing her grief over their dear departed friend.

That night, it seems the entire army celebrates. Various animals are butchered in great numbers for a tremendous feast, complete with song and dance. While Danahlia is taken around to be welcomed home by her people, Alice sits alone with Squiggles in the clearing. He has not been left out of the celebration and has been given an ample supply of meats. Even so, even he has trouble enjoying them, knowing something, if not precisely what, is wrong with Alice. He nuzzles under her arm like he did when he was much smaller, but his head if so large now that even stretching, Alice can only reach the top of his nose. She pets him while looking blankly at the bowl of food she had been given. She knew it smelled wonderful and that she was quite hungry, but couldn't seem to muster the energy to eat from it.

Danahlia eventually manages to break away from the celebration to join her.

"Ya know, chances are Twinkie 'll figure out she's too short to do anythin' without us and 'll come right back begging us to go with 'er," the Liguna says encouragingly, "She's smart like that."

Alice gives her a forced smile but it fades quickly.

"Plus, your dad 'll be here soon. Maybe after we pick 'im up, we can go look for 'er," Danahlia tries again.

"Maybe," Alice says without looking up, "If it

really is him."

"It's gotta be," assures Danahlia, giving Alice a hug, "If my uncle says it is, it is. You'll see."

"You don't really wanna leave do you?" Alice asks, "You're finally back home, with your own kind."

Danahlia considers, "Yeah, that's true. But," she says burying her face into the fur of Alice's cheek, "It's way more fun adventurin' with you guys." Danahlia suddenly stops, "Oh, ticks, we gotta go check on Kali, she must be freakin' by now with all the crumb snatchers." Managing to rouse Alice to action, the girls make a plan.

Once Alice has her father or not, they will all go back to Arsalia. They will find Kaliska and bring her and the children back to Feoria to live out the war under Danahlia's Uncle's protection. If they're swift they're sure the Order will not be able to catch up to them. Once the children are safe, they will begin their search for Twinkaleni. It's not a very detailed plan but it comforts Alice greatly to have something to look forward to.

For several days, Alice and Danahlia are kept in Danahlia's uncle's base. No great battles erupt between the two formidable forces leering at one another from across the Elois. According to Javas, this is how the majority of the war has been spent on this front. Both sides simply fortifying their positions while stretching along the river banks as they probe for weaknesses in the others defenses. Occasionally, a minor skirmish will flare up, but for the most part, they only try to wait each other out, neither force willing to surrender this critical passage into their lands. Danahlia's uncle says his niece's return has been the only thing worth celebrating in a long boring while. He laughs when he says after they saw Squiggles flying over to join their camp, the Warm Bloods are even less likely to start any trouble now.

On yet another particularly unremarkable morning, Alice and Danahlia are playing with Squiggles, riding his tail as he swings it about and scratching him in the places he likes. Someone clears their throat behind Alice and when she turns, Javas and his two guards are standing a few yards away. Between them is a male Tokala.

The man is thin, ragged, and his fur is a dirty

mess. He looks awe struck and open mouthed at the dragon before him. Alice's immediate impression is that he is far too short to be her father, but another hopeful little thought tells her that she hadn't seen him in a very long time, she was much smaller then. Curiously, she approaches and only once feet from him does she take his attention. His eyes widen even more when he spots her and Alice can see something very familiar in those eyes, sky blue like her own. Her body wants to crumble to the ground as a very faint, almost frightened whisper escapes her.

"Daddy?"

Epilogue

Alice and her father are kept in Feoria under Danahlia's uncle's protection, Javas Ashclaw not wanting to risk letting one of Arsalia's greatest warriors go, only to rejoin the war effort against his people. Robert Dippleblack agrees to this and Alice and her father are kept not as prisoners but as guests with their own house deep in Feorian territory within the walls of one of their greater cities. For this, Javas also wants Robert the Red to teach his men his sword techniques so they may better face them in the field. Robert Dippleblack agrees to this also, with the concession that his daughter is allowed to learn as well.

Alice, also not allowed to return to Arsalia as per her father and Javas' agreement, is parted from Danahlia when the Liguna travels with Squiggles to Arsalia to carry out their plans. Her uncle doesn't like it but even he will not argue with a dragon. Several weeks later, Danahlia returns with only Perthi and the news that Kaliska and the children are fine and being helped by the Cloudstalkers, the tribe of bird people having returned to the mountains for the winter. Kaliska and the other children, having nothing to fear of the Order, decide to stay where they are to continue their efforts of saving the orphans of the Blood War. Danahlia continues to make trips to check on Kaliska and the children as well as see if Twinkaleni has stopped by, though the answer is always no.

Alice spends two years in Feoria with her father until a particularly lengthy and harsh winter has the warring nations calling for a temporary cease fire. When spring finally arrives, both sides have lost interest in resuming the war and a shaky peace is allowed to begin. To give the peace strength, many marriages are arranged between prominent Cold Blood clans and Warm Blood houses, Danahlia's among them. For the peace between the nations, Danahlia agrees to the mostly symbolic union of herself and a rather handsome, young, Echanian noble.

The Blood War finally at an end, Alice and her father are freed to return home to Arsalia. They fly atop Squiggles first to see Kaliska. In her enthusiasm to magically heal those in need of it, the Chitali has managed to build a bit of a reputation for herself in the far northern town of Borea, one of the larger settlements the girls had traded with during their time in the Gadara Mountains. Grateful, and sometimes wealthy, patrons would donate to the deer girl's cause and eventually she was able to buy a small house for her and the children under her care, turning it into a true orphanage. From there she would continue her divine mission that she insists was given to her by the Goddess Althea.

Alice and her father then travel to the little town of Toki, where Alice had grown up. Squiggles is left in the pixie forest nearby and the reunited father and daughter pay their respects to Alice's mother's resting place. Alice then makes her way to the local trading post. She finds her old friend, Ashleigh Graysen, there running it with her mother just like when she first left. After a fond embrace, the Didel girl is more eager than ever to hear all about Alice's grand adventures.

Even through all of this, Alice would always find her thoughts returning to her tiny Murin friend, mostly at night when there was little to distract her mind. She wonders if she still lived, and if so, where? She wonders if the mage had ever tried to free her kind again from the awful Order of Thermathrogi and how she would manage it, now all alone. She often found herself coming to tears, thinking of how Twinkaleni was by herself, so small and still so young, without even the aid of her friends to help in her monumental undertaking.

In the years since parting company, Alice had heard nothing of Twinkaleni, not even rumors, and it would be years more before she would...

About the Author:

K.J. Bailey (Kenichiro Justin Bailey) has thus far only written the Alice Dippleblack series, but looks forward to creating more fantastical worlds.